THE HARD HITTER

CATHRYN FOX

COPYRIGHT

Copyright 2018 by Cathryn Fox
Published by Cathryn Fox

people. If you would like to share this book with another person, please purchase an additional copy for each recipient. If you're reading this book and did not purchase it, or it was not purchased for your use only, then please return to your favorite e-book retailer and purchase your own copy. Thank you for respecting the hard work of this author.

Discover other titles by Cathryn Fox at www.cathrynfox.com. Please sign up for Cathryn's Newsletter for freebies, ebooks, news and contests:
https://app.mailerlite.com/webforms/landing/c1f8n1
ISBN ebook 978-1-928056-99-7
Print: 978-1-989374-00-9

1

ZANDER

As I drive through the busy Friday afternoon traffic, I glance in the rearview mirror and grimace when I catch my sweet daughter Daisy's reflection. I love my daughter more than life, but if she keeps singing that damn alligator song and chomping her hands together, my brain is going to explode into a million tiny pieces. Have you ever seen that scene from *Pulp Fiction* where John Travolta's character Vincent accidently shoots Lamarr in the backseat of the car? Brains everywhere. Yeah, any second now, and we're pretty much going to have a reenactment of that.

Okay, okay, I get it. The alligator song is about teaching kids pattern recognition, and it's great for auditory skills and expressive language. That's all well and fine. But what is it teaching us parents? Oh, my guess would be how to find the bottom of a scotch bottle sooner rather than later.

"Hey Daisy," I say, and she puts her toy iPad down and blinks up at me. "Did you have fun at daycare today?"

Her head bobs emphatically, and my heart beats a little harder in my chest as her dark lashes blink rapidly over big blue eyes. How her mother could have just dropped her tiny four-month-old baby on my buddy Jonah's doorstep a few years ago is beyond me. What kind of woman uses a child to trap a guy? As if that wasn't bad enough, Daisy wasn't even Jonah's child to begin with.

No, she was mine. We found that out later when her secret plan to marry Jonah backfired on her. Now she's nowhere to be found, and I have full custody of my little girl.

Nevertheless, back when it happened, Jonah stepped up to be the man the little girl needed. In the end, he had a hard time handing Daisy over to me when the truth came out, but that doesn't mean he's not a part of her life anymore. Not only is he my best friend, he married my sister Quinn, and now he's Uncle Jonah to Daisy.

"Daddy," she says, and reaches for her doll. "I want to play with Scotty."

Th-snotty.

I chuckle at that, even though I shouldn't. Daisy has a hard time with her s's, which I why we're currently on our way to Andover to see the speech pathologist my sister Quinn recommended. I also shouldn't laugh because she's calling her one-year-old cousin 'snotty.' Although with the allergies he's been suffering from lately, that's not too far off from the truth.

I glance at my GPS, and turn right as I enter an older suburb of Andover, a good forty-minute drive from our home in Cambridge. I slow down as kids run up and down the sidewalk, some kicking a ball, others using chalk on the driveways. I glance at the house numbers and when I find the one I'm looking for, I slow down and pull up to the curb.

"We can't play with Scotty today, because we're going to see that nice lady Samantha. Remember I told you about her?"

"But I want to play with Scotty."

"You played with him all morning, honey, and will see him

again tomorrow." My sister Quinn owns her own daycare, and while I'd like to keep Daisy with me during the daytime, next year she starts kindergarten, and I know the interaction is good for her. Playing for the Seattle Shooters means being on the road during hockey season. I don't like to give up any time with Daisy during my summer breaks, but I need to do what's best for my child.

I turn the car off and climb from the driver's seat. Daisy is already unbuckling herself by the time I open her door. I love her fierce independence. Truly, I do. But God help me when she becomes a teen.

Abandoning her toys, she slides her tiny palm into mine, and I help her from her car seat. I honestly have no idea how this session is going to go, or what I'm supposed to do or expect, but Samantha was recommended by Quinn, so I'm willing to make the long commute and put my child's care in her hands.

"All set?" I ask, and hit the fob to lock the car.

I slow my steps to match hers as we make our way up the cracked and pitted walkway. It's an older home, as many of them are in this suburb. I pull Daisy close so she doesn't brush up against the car in the small driveway.

Daisy clings to my leg, and while she's not normally nervous around strangers, I sense her worry. I explained this whole meeting to her, but she's too young to really understand. I pick her up and she cups my cheeks with her hands.

"Daddy, you look like Andi," she says, and she squeezes my cheeks together and laughs. Andi is her goldfish, and no way do we look alike.

"Oh, is that right?" I ask, and tickle her sides as I make goldfish lips and move my mouth, not the most attractive look, I know. I play with her like that for a minute, until a voice interrupts us.

"Hi."

Lips still puckered, I go perfectly still—and shift my gaze to see the hottest woman on the planet, holding her door open and trying to bite back a grin.

Shit.

I stop puckering, and she extends her hand to me. "You must be Zander."

"I am," I say and slide my hand into hers, taking note of her softness, the light, sweet vanilla scent of her skin. It reminds me of the icing we used on the cupcakes last night.

She turns her attention to Daisy. "And you must be Daisy," she says, and produces an alligator puppet from behind her back.

Daisy giggles and reaches for the alligator. "Chomp. Chomp," she squeals.

"I...uh..." I begin. "I take it you're Samantha?"

"I am. You can call me Sam," she says, as I stand there like an idiot and try to think of something intelligent to say.

This gorgeous woman is Sam, the speech pathologist? When Quinn gave me her name and set up the appointment for us, I never for one second thought Sam would be young and beautiful. The vision in my mind was one of an older lady, grey hair, tall and slender, a strict disciplinarian with kids. But holy hell, this is no Nanny McPhee. Quite the opposite actually.

As she uses her puppet to nibble on Daisy's toes, I take that moment to look her over. Yeah, okay, I know, I know. I should not be ogling my daughter's speech pathologist. It's been a long time since I've been with a woman, and this one —with her long dark hair piled high in a ponytail, her fresh girl-next-door looks, and curves to die for—quickly remind me of that. It's not that I've been off women. I just had other, more important matters at hand. Like taking care of Daisy, being careful who I bring into her life, and playing hard for the Shooters.

Oh shit, she's saying something to me.

I scratch my chin. "Ah, what was that?"

"Come on in," she says and steps back to give us room to enter.

I step inside and set Daisy down. When I turn back I note the way Sam is struggling to get her screen door shut. "Need a hand?"

"I got it. I just have to give it a good hard tug. I think it's the hinges. I haven't had a chance to fix them yet."

She fixes her own hinges?

Does that mean she doesn't have a man in her life? Not that a woman needs a man to do her handiwork, and I'm sure she's quite capable herself...but dammit, I'd love to get my hands on her hinges, slide them right into place for her.

She gets the door closed and turns to us. A smile lights up her face as she zeroes in on Daisy, and I already feel the connection between the two. She's obviously great with kids. She holds her hand out to my daughter.

"Daisy, would you like to see my playroom?"

Daisy nods her head but sticks close to me. I give her a nudge to let her know it's okay, and she takes Sam's hand. Two ponytails bounce as I follow behind, and I go quiet as Sam engages my daughter in conversation, no doubt to gauge her lisp. I glance into the living room as we pass and take in her bookshelf, small TV, and soft leather sofa and chair. The place is small compared to mine, but homey, and I like that.

My own place is too large for just Daisy and me. Quinn insists I fill it with more kids, and I insists she's crazy. Truthfully, I'm not about to bring anyone into my life who could possibly hurt Daisy. We've both had enough people run out on us.

Yeah, it's clear I'm jaded where women are concerned.

But can you blame me? My own mom left when Quinn and I were little and much of the responsibly of raising my younger sister landed on me—not that I'm complaining. Toss in a puck bunny who used Daisy to snag herself a hockey player, and then gave up custody when her plan backfired. On top of that, my girlfriend left me when she discovered Daisy was mine. She wasn't prepared for a ready-made family, and just up and left without so much as a backward glance.

Yeah, I'm a cynic when it comes to long term. No one ever sticks around. But sex and relationships are two different beasts, and this woman is reminding me it's been too long since I breathed in sweet-smelling skin, found myself between a soft pair of thighs.

We go down the hall and step into a room, likely a former bedroom, that has been converted to an office.

"Why don't you go check out the toys," she says to Daisy. Daisy bounces off, and Sam straightens. She has a soft pink flush on her face when she turns back to me. "Excuse the mess."

"Looks perfectly good to me," I say as I catalogue the room.

"It's probably not what you expected." She waves her hand. "But I'm hoping to break that wall down and put a door in the...the..." She pauses for a second, like she's trying to gather herself, then says, "I would like for the office to have direct access to the outside, so clients won't have to go through my home."

"Have you been here long?" I ask.

"No, just a couple months, and just getting set up. I really appreciate Quinn sending work my way."

Daisy squeals when she finds some orange stuffed bear, and Sam gestures to a chair. "Please have a seat so we can get the consultation underway, then if it's okay with you, I'll ask you to have a seat in the living room, so I can have one-on-one time with Daisy." She opens a file, and slides a paper across the desk. I glance it over, fill in my information, including my insurance, and lift my head to slide it back.

When I do, I find Sam watching me. Her eyes go wide and she tears her gaze away fast, then goes about fussing with the papers.

"I...uh...okay." She closes the file, takes another breath like she's trying to center herself again, and says, "Everything looks in order."

"Do you think you can help her?" I ask.

A warm smile comes over her face as she turns her focus to Daisy. "I'll do my best." She stands and I follow her up. "We'll take it slow. Best not to rush things or put too much pressure on her." Her big brown eyes narrow. "Have you been working with her at home, trying to get her to enunciate properly?"

I reach behind me and rub the back of my neck. "Uh, not really. Should I have been doing that?" I ask. Dammit, I guess I'm not about to win any father of the year awards here.

As if sensing my unease, Sam puts her hand on my arm. "Oh, no. Not at all. There will be exercises later, but right now it's best not to put pressure on her."

"Whew," I say and exhale loudly. That brings a smile to her face. I lower my voice. "I just don't want to screw up with her, you know?" I gaze at my daughter as she talks to the stuffed orange bear. "It's just her and me, and I don't always know if I'm making the right choices."

"I understand," Sam says quietly, and I shake my head.

Why am I telling her this? Then again, I'm guessing if she's a friend of Quinn's, she's well-versed in the situation that made me a single dad. I'm about to leave the room, take a seat in her living room, when her voice stops me.

"You're not what I expected," she blurts out, then her eyes go wide again, like she said something she shouldn't have.

"What did you expect?" I ask.

"I...I..." She laughs, but it's strained and uneasy. "I'm sorry, Zander. I shouldn't have said that. That wasn't professional."

I put my hands into my pockets and her gaze drops for a brief second as my jeans sink lower on my hips. "For the record, you're not what I expected, either."

"What did *you* expect?" she asked, her eyes flying back to mine.

"Nanny McPhee," I say, and her mouth drops open.

"Are you serious?" I nod. "Why?" she asks.

"Beats me," I say, as my thoughts stray, turn to the bedroom, and all the things I'd like to do with her beneath the sheets.

Okay, dude. Cool it. You are not, under any circumstance, going to have your way with your daughter's speech pathologist, no matter how hot she is.

"Well, I'm sorry to disappoint you," she says quietly, in a very non-flirtatious manner that makes me want to play with her, tease her a little.

"I never said I was disappointed," I return, my voice lower, deeper.

Stop flirting already.

She draws her bottom lip between her teeth as the color on her cheeks deepen. She points to the door. "There are some magazines on the coffee table to help you pass the time."

I reach for the door, needing the distraction. "Thanks."

She bites back a grin. "I was going to suggest you practice your goldfish lips, but you've already nailed that.

Nailed that.

I laugh at her joke, but deep between my legs, my cock is jumping at her choice of words. Damned if I don't want to show the hot speech pathologist how good I am with my words, too.

2
SAM

Holy mother of all that is hot.

I had no idea my friend's brother was such a hottie. I only knew the hockey player they call the 'Hard Hitter' by reputation. Unlike my hockey-obsessed father, I don't follow the game and was ill prepared to come face to face with that panty-melting smile of his. I shouldn't have blurted out that he wasn't what I expected—sometimes my mouth works faster than my brain, which has gotten me in trouble in the past.

Truthfully, I expected an egomaniac, a guy who strutted around like he was the cock of the walk. What I found instead was a guy who cared about his daughter's well-being. A guy whose words made my thoughts go in a direction I didn't want then to go. I'm off men for a while, maybe even forever. A relationship is not in my near future, considering how many of them I've screwed up in the past. Now I'm all work and no play, my business my main concern.

How's that working out for you, Sam?

Not great, judging by the way my body reacted when faced with six feet of pure testosterone. A hot, dominant male with calloused hands that have undoubtedly brought a lot of pleasure.

I take a deep, steady breath and pull myself together as my office door closes with a soft click. Even though he's gone, his scent—that of freshly showered skin—and his presence still dominate the small space. Working to clear my thoughts and get my much-neglected body under control, I turn my attention to sweet little Daisy as she happily babbles with the bear. Zander might be the hottest guy I've ever seen, but I'm not about to spend this session thinking about him.

But later...when I'm tucked into bed. Oh, how I'll imagine all the dirty things he says between the sheets, all the filthy things he'll demand of me.

Stop it, Sam!

Good God. I'm a professional, and getting involved with a client's parent is anything but smart. Not that I think I'm his type or anything. He probably dates perfect women. Perfect hair, perfect bodies, perfect speech...perfectly proper.

While I might come across as that nice girl, deep down I have cravings...needs. Not that I'd ever express them. Not ever again, anyway. It was less than a year ago, after I'd blurted out in bed that I wanted it a bit rough, that my fiancé went ballistic. He made me feel small, embarrassed, saying there was something wrong with me. Nice girls like me shouldn't want such filth. He was disgusted with me, and when I tried to explain, my damn stutter came back, making me feel twice as foolish.

He'd looked at me with disdain, his lips twisted in derision. I'll never forget the way he made me feel. Never want to feel that way again. After he dumped me, broke off the engagement, I locked up my longings, buried my cravings, and put my focus into my business.

Truthfully, when it comes to relationships, I have a penchant for ruining them. Before my fiancé, I once blurted out that I loved the guy I'd been seeing. That sent him running. And before him, the guy I'd been dating said I didn't pay him enough attention. I'd been studying too much, apparently, and failed to create work/life/balance.

Yeah, I'm a screw up.

Now, relationships are not on my agenda. Since I can't quite figure out the whole balance thing, my entire focus is on work—growing my business so I can pay down my student loans and still make my mortgage payments.

"Daisy, I see you found Mr. Giggles."

"Mr. Giggles," she says her 's' coming out at a 'th'.

I drop down onto the floor next to her and for the next half hour, spend some time getting to know her. From the other room, I hear my front door open, the screen door clanging shut. I'm guessing Daisy's father must have gotten bored with the magazines and decided to get a breath of fresh air. Not that I can blame him. It's a beautiful day. I spend the rest of our time practicing a few more enunciation games with Daisy, then climb to my feet.

"Want to go see what Daddy's up to?" I ask her.

She gives me a smile and nods her head. "Daddy said he would get me an ice cream later."

I check my watch. It's late afternoon, and Daisy was my last client of the day. "Well aren't you a lucky girl." I open the door to the office. "What's your favorite kind of ice cream?"

"Chocolate."

A girl after my own heart. "Me too," I say and lead her down the hall.

But when I spot Zander at my front door, screwdriver in his hand and fixing my hinges, I stop dead in my tracks.

"What...what are you doing?" I ask.

He glances at me over his shoulder, his eyes lingering a moment too long, then he grins and says, "Fixing your door. I hope you don't mind?"

"You didn't have to do that."

"What can I say, I was bored. When I'm bored, I like to put my hands to use."

Before I can help myself, my gaze drops to his hands—big, calloused hands—and my thoughts race, thinking about other ways he might put those hands to use...on my body. Roughly.

Oh, God...

"Daddy, the big bear is named Mr. Giggles," Daisy says and chuckles.

"Is that right?" Zander asks, and holds his arms out for his daughter. She darts toward him, and he scoops her up. "Did you have fun?" She nods her head, and her ponytail bounces around her tiny shoulders.

Zander looks at me, his eyes holding so many questions.

"She did just fine," I say. I step closer and tap Daisy on the nose. But when I do, tension arcs between Zander and me.

Holy! Never in my life have I felt such electricity, such deep desire stirring in my body. This kind of thing never happens to me. Nevertheless, I'd be smart to ignore it. I can't let anything distract me from my business. Not when I'm in the danger zone. All my focus and energy must go into my career, getting it in the black so I can start paying things down.

"I guess I should book another appointment."

"Same time next week?" I ask. Then again, maybe he has better things to do on a late Friday afternoon. Like get ready for a hot date or something. "Unless you have plans," I say.

He thinks about it for a second, then nods. "No plans. That will work."

"We're getting ice cream," Daisy says.

"That's right. Those are our big plans for the night."

"Sam likes chocolate too. Daddy likes vanilla, but I don't."

"Vanilla is good," he says, his nostrils flaring, like he can smell the body wash I showered with earlier.

"Can Sam come with us?"

Zander's gaze shoots to mine. "Uh..."

"Thanks for asking, Daisy. But I'm not able to come," I say. "I have plans." Not really a lie. I have a meal that needs to go in the microwave and a date with Netflix.

Zander gives a curt nod. "We'll get out of your way then."

He's about to leave but stops when I say, "Thank you for fixing my door. I really appreciate it. Can I pay you for it?"

His eyes narrow, like he's surprised by that. "It was nothing. But maybe..."

"Maybe what?"

He scrubs his chin, looks at his daughter as she cups his cheeks, and then shakes his head, as if to get it on right. Is he changing his mind about what he was going to say? He winks at me. "Maybe a cup of coffee or something next time I'm by."

My cheeks heat, mortified. My God, my mother would kill me for my bad manners. I always offer a beverage to the parents. But this time I was so thrown off by his good looks and charm—the way he dominated my space—my manners packed a bag and headed south...meeting up with my suddenly overactive libido.

"I'm...I'm so sorry," I say. *Don't stutter Sam.* "Excuse my bad manners."

His smile falls. "No, no. It's okay. I was just kidding. I had a coffee in the car on the way here."

Okay, so if he was teasing about the coffee, what was he really going to say?

Oh, maybe you can make it up to me with a hot, dirty roll in the sack, where I hold you down hard and give it to you even harder.

My entire body buzzes to life.

"Ice cream, Daddy," Daisy sings out, breaking the tension. Zander smiles at his daughter.

"Ice cream it is." He gives me a nod and walks through the

door. The screen glides shut behind him, and I open it and close it again, checking out his handiwork. He's a hockey player, good with a stick, but I guess I never took him for a handyman, too. From what Quinn told me, after their mother walked out on them when they were young, their father worked long hours as a mail carrier and wasn't there much for the family. A lot of the responsibility fell on Zander.

As my thoughts go to Quinn, I grab my cell from my back pocket and send her a text.

Zander and Daisy just left.

Three dots repeat as she texts back.

How did it go?

Great, Daisy is a sweetie.

I stare at the phone as she texts back, debating my next words.

She really is. Zander is doing a great job with her.

Speaking of Zander...

Your brother is nice.

I leave out the hotter-than-hell part. Best not to give Quinn any ideas. I haven't known her that long—we met a couple years back, after she started her own daycare and was searching for a speech pathologist—but she's always trying to set me up. I had just graduated when she first reached out to me, working at a clinic to gain experience. We hit it off, but she's always at me—*you need to date, Sam. You need to get out more.*

She's not wrong.

He fixed my door.

That was nice of him.

Like I said, he's nice. I'd like to repay him. Any ideas how?

Three little dots pop up again, and I fully expect her to come back with something inappropriate. Then again, maybe not. This is, after all, her big brother.

He likes pie.

I stare at that for a moment and wonder what she's getting at. *Pie?* I text back. Where the hell is she going with this?

Yeah, homemade. Especially cherry.

Are you suggesting I make him a cherry pie?

And deliver it to him. He's home with Daisy tonight. I'll send you his address.

I ignore the odd little thrill that he's not on some hot date.

Don't you think that's a bit much?

No.

His address comes through, and I do a double take. He's in one hell of a posh area of Cambridge. Then again, it shouldn't surprise me. He's a hockey player worth millions. I can't imagine what he thought of my rundown little place, or what he'd think of the small house I'd grown up in. It wasn't much, but I had the love and support of my mother and father.

Gotta run, Scotty is crying.

I slide my finger across the phone and end the call. Turning, I stare down the hall and into my kitchen.

Wait, I'm not really considering Quinn's suggestion, am I? How weird would it be to find myself on Zander's doorstep with a cherry pie in hand—a homemade cherry pie. I do make a mean one, having spent a lot of time in the kitchen baking with Mom when I was young.

The man fixed my door. A cherry pie to thank him is overkill, and he'd probably think I was crazy. Okay, enough of that. I am not going to bake him a pie and deliver it. No way. No how.

I don't think.

3

ZANDER

I step from a hot shower and wrap a towel around my waist. As I saunter to my room to tug on a pair of clean jeans, I glance in and smile when I see my daughter sleeping soundly in her pink convertible bed, a gurgling sound coming from the fish tank in the corner.

My heart wobbles a bit as I stare at her. I really want to do right by her, and give her the world. I know I can be an overprotective dick at times, but that's just part of who I am. It's important to me that I don't make the mistakes my parents made—leaving us to fend for ourselves—yet I don't want to turn her into one of those self-entitled children I see in the parks and at Quinn's daycare. It's a balancing act for sure, and I've read all the books. Still, there is no one answer. Every child is different.

I pull her door, leaving it open an inch, and pad quietly to my room. I'm about to drop my towel when my doorbell rings.

Who the fuck would be at my house this time of night?

I glance at the clock on my nightstand and shake my head. Fuck, I'm twenty-nine, and now I consider eight o'clock late. Shit, whatever happened to the guy who stayed out all night, partied endlessly with the puck bunnies?

He grew up.

Yeah, he grew up in a hurry, especially after finding out he had a daughter to raise, single-handedly. Well not really. I do have Quinn and Jonah.

I drop my towel and hurry into a pair of jeans. Foregoing a shirt, I race down the stairs and make my way to the front door. I yank it open—

And find Sam on my stoop, a pie in her hand.

I stand there for a second, my brain racing to catch up. She blinks up at me, arousing the animal in me.

Am I hallucinating? If not, what the fuck is going on?

"Hi," Sam says, breaking the awkward silence. "I was talking to Quinn, and she said cherry was your favorite." She holds the pie out and my stomach grumbles. Tonight's dinner consisted of grilled-cheese sandwiches—and that was hours ago.

But why is Sam bringing me pie?

As if reading my mind she says, "I wanted to thank you for fixing my door."

Ah.

"You didn't have to go through the trouble." Her smile falls, and she takes a small step backward, the pink flush crawling up her neck making her look so adorable. She opens her mouth, but I cut her off and say, "But I'm glad you did."

Her smile returns, and it's like a punch to the gut. My God, she's gorgeous. Which begs the question, why is she home baking a pie for me on a Friday night, and not on some hot date?

"It smells delicious."

She beams up at me. "It tastes even better than it smells."

"You made it?"

She nods. "My mother's secret recipe."

"The kind of secret where if you tell me, you'd have to kill me." She laughs at that, and I wave my hand toward my hall. "Then let's see if you're right."

"Oh, I wasn't..."

"You don't know the pie rules?" I ask, before I can second-guess what I'm doing. Christ, I haven't had a woman in my home, other than my sister or Daisy's nanny, for years now.

She crinkles her nose and shifts from one foot to the other. "There are pie rules?"

"Sure. If someone makes you a pie, you have to have the first slice together. If you don't, you'll have seven years of bad luck."

She plants on hand on her hip. "You're making that up. Seven years bad luck comes from breaking a mirror."

"Well, if you're willing to risk the streak of bad luck... I know I'm not." I keep the smile from my face as she eyes me. Probably trying to decide if I'm kidding or some kind of weirdo. "Scouts honor," I add for good measure, and because I never was a scout, I'm not really lying. Wait, does that even make sense?

"Fine, I don't need any bad luck either," she says and walks through the threshold. She stops a few feet inside, and my gaze lands on her ass as I close the door behind us. She looks to her left, then to her right, taking in my place.

"Sorry about the mess," I say. I hadn't had a chance to clean up after Daisy tonight.

"It's not messy. It's homey," she says and turns back to me, a small smile on her face. Her gaze leaves mine and drops to my bare upper body. "I...uh...you..."

"What?" I ask.

She takes a deep breath, a gesture that is becoming famil-iar, and says, "If you point me to the kitchen, I'll cut the pie so you can go put a shirt on."

Is my near nakedness throwing her off?

If so, maybe I shouldn't put a shirt on.

Dude, get it together. You are not sleeping with this girl. Enough that you brought her into the house.

"Yeah, okay." I take her shoulders, and her entire body goes tight when I spin her around. She sucks in a fast breath, and the tension in her body travels all the way to my dick, gives it a nice slow stroke. Fuck, man, if I knew she was going to show up at my door, I would have tugged one out in the shower so I wouldn't be so tempted. Everything about this girl brings out the animal in me, and reminds me I haven't had a good hard fuck in ages.

I hurry upstairs and tug on a shirt. I rake my hands through my mess of hair to smooth it down and by the time I get back downstairs, Sam is placing two slices of pie on the table.

"Damn, that looks good." She dips her finger into the sauce and brings it to her mouth. She makes a moaning sound, and my cock jumps in my pants.

Motherfucker. This is going to be a long, *hard* night.

"Good, huh?" I ask. Shit, is that my voice?

"Delicious."

"I can't wait to try it."

I take a step toward her and she pulls a chair back for me. "Then have a seat."

"How about a drink?"

"Sure."

"Wine okay?" For some reason, she strikes me as the wine type.

"If it's no trouble."

"No trouble at all," I say and pull a chilled bottle of white from the fridge. Quinn brought it the last time she came for dinner. I uncork it, and Sam sits there with her hands on her lap, waiting patiently for me to join her at the table. I kind of like that she hasn't dug into her pie. She has great manners, and that makes my thoughts stray to the bedroom. Everything in me tells me she's prim and proper, a nice girl. But I get the sense that her tastes match mine behind closed doors.

I pour wine into two glasses and hand her the stemware. I hold mine up for a toast, and say cheers. She averts her gaze, goes to clink glasses, and I stop her.

"Wait, are you telling me that you don't know the rules of toasting?"

Her brow furrows and she gives me a suspicious look. "What's with you and all the rules?" she asks. "You don't strike me as the kind of guy who follows many."

I laugh at that. "Well, this is an important rule. You have to make eye contact after clinking glasses and before drinking."

"And if I don't?"

"Bad sex for seven years."

Her big brown eyes go wide. "You're making that up."

"Look it up," I say and gesture to my laptop on the kitchen counter.

"Fine, I will." She grabs my laptop, opens it and hands it to me to type in my password. Typing fast, she does a quick search...and starts laughing. "Oh my God, you're right!" She turns the computer for me to see. "Apparently there are five reasons to make eye contact, and number three is seven years of bad sex. How did you even know about that?"

She closes the laptop and reaches for her wine glass again, like she's ready to give it a second try.

I give her a sheepish look. "I think I might have too much time on my hands after putting Daisy to bed."

"Maybe you need a hobby." She shrugs. "Earlier today, you said when you're bored you like to put your hands to use. Perhaps in the evenings, you need something to occupy your hands," she says casually.

My mind takes that moment to imagine my hands on her body, touching her in all the ways I've wanted to since first setting eyes on her.

I swallow. Hard. I take my glass in my hand and lift it. There is such an innocent quality about her, I'm not sure she meant those words to be sexual, but something tells me she'd like my dirty brand of sex. My brain takes that moment to expand on those filthy thoughts, twisting them in my head until my cock grows another inch.

"Cheers," I say, and her big brown eyes meet mine. The second our gazes lock, hold a minute too long, hunger rips through me. Fuck, man, I want this woman in my bed. Simple as that. It might not be wise or smart, but there it is. I want my hands and mouth on her body.

"Cheers," she says, and keeps her eyes on mine as she brings the glass to her mouth for a swallow. She pulls the glass away and licks he moisture from her bottom lip. "This is delicious."

"Yeah, delicious," I say, my mind on other things. I take a drink and set my glass down.

"Tell me what you think," she says.

I'm about to open my mouth and tell her *exactly* what I think when she gestures to the pie.

"Tell me that's not the best thing you've ever put in your mouth."

Jesus, the speech pathologist is killing me with her words.

Damned if I don't want to do the same to her. How would she react if I let loose, told her what I really wanted, holding nothing back? Would she run the other way, or would the sweet girl next door like the way I use my mouth?

I pick up my fork, cut into the flaky pie, and slide it into my mouth. Flavor explodes on my tongue. I swallow and wash it down with a drink. Sam sits beside me, waiting for my response.

I cut another piece and bring it to my mouth. "I think you've ruined me," I say before eating.

"Ruined you?"

I chew and swallow. "I'll never be able to eat cherry pie again. They'll all pale in comparison."

She chuckles softly. "Does that mean I'm going to have to keep you in cherry pie for the rest of your life?"

"Yeah, I think so."

"Well, how about this, as long as I'm working with Daisy, I'll make you all the cherry pie you want." She shrugs. "I actually enjoy baking, and it's nice to have someone to bake for again." As if she said too much, her head rears back. "I mean...I just...I used to bake with my mom when I was younger, and I..."

"That's nice, Sam," I say, coming to her rescue. "You were close to your mom?"

She nods. "Still am."

My heart wobbles at that. She had the kind of upbringing I wanted for Quinn, still want for Daisy.

"I'm close to Dad, too." She takes a big bite of pie, like she's trying to fill her mouth before she blurts out something else. I think it's adorable, actually, and can't help but wonder what she'd say, how she'd react if I blurted out all the dirty thoughts pinging around inside my brain.

I finish the pie and drain my glass. Standing, I bring the bottle back to the table and pour more into her glass first.

"I won't be able to drink that. I'm driving," she says.

"Then I guess you'll just have to stay a bit longer." I pour more into my glass and take her empty plate away.

"It's late. I should probably go." She stands, and our bodies bump. She sucks in a fast breath, and there's no way she's not feeling this crazy sexual tension between us. Her cheeks are a deeper shade of pink, and the black in her eyes had bled into the brown. Whether she wants to admit it or not, she's as aroused as I am.

"What's the hurry, Sam? It's Friday night and it's still early enough. Maybe you could stick around, help me figure out how to keep my hands busy." Our fingers brush, and she makes a soft, sexy bedroom sound that cups my balls and massages gently.

"I...I..."

"If you want to go, no problem," I say causally, even though there is a storm of want roiling through me. "But you should know..." I pause, and wait to see if she takes the bait.

"Know what?"

"I'm not so sure you were right about the pie?"

"Not right about it. What do you mean?"

"I think there might something else in the running for the best things I've ever put in my mouth. But I'd have to taste it first to be sure."

4
SAM

Ohmigod. Did he just say what I think he said? Or is my sexually frustrated body interpreting his words wrong. Flabbergasted, and unsure of what's really going on here, I falter backward, but he slides his hand around my body and brings me close, close enough for me to feel the missile between his legs.

Alrighty then.

In a bold move, completely uncharacteristic of me, I move against him slightly, take measure of what he's working with.

A growl catches in his throat and snaps me back to reality. I blink quickly, shake my head to get it on right. I look past his shoulders, toward the front hall. I should go, get in my car and drive away, never to set eyes on this hot guy again. Not only is he my friend's brother, he's a client's father, and everything about him makes me want to be bad...dirty...something a good girl like me should never want, right?

I should run, but can't seem to pull myself away from the thickness between his legs. As heat zings through my body and dampens my panties, I open my mouth to tell him this isn't a good idea, but instead, I find myself saying, "What exactly is it that you have to taste first?"

Holy God.

He grins at that. The hot, dirty-talking hockey player is actually grinning at my question. Probably because he knows he's got me right where he wants me, and the truth is, I'm right where I want to be too, because dammit, it's time I had some much-needed fun.

Tomorrow, I'll set him and Daisy up with a new pathologist—one with more experience than me. It's a win-win, right?

Oh, who am I kidding, this is all kinds of wrong, and there isn't a thing I can to do stop it, not when he's running his thick index finger over my lips and looking at me like he's going to devour me whole.

Yes, please.

"This mouth," he begins. "These lips." He dips his head and brushes his mouth over mine, so softly, my entire body quivers. "Do you have any idea what I wanted to do to this mouth of yours since I first set eyes on you today?"

"No," I say, hanging on his every word and hoping they get dirtier. Good God, what is going on with me? I'm a good girl who shouldn't want—crave—to hear filthy words. But my ears are perked up, wanting just that. I move against his body, rub my softness against his hardness, and he puts him mouth to my ear, his growl vibrating through me.

"I nearly tugged one out in the shower as I pictured you on your knees before me. You worshipping my cock as I fed it to you."

"Zander," I say quickly, his name slipping from my lips.

"Yeah, you like the idea of that?"

"I..." *Be honest, Sam. Take a chance.*

As I think about that, the humiliation of last time hits like a sucker punch.

"Do you?" he asks again, a little more force behind his words. I lift my eyes to his, and his gaze searches my face.

He knows! He knows how I want it—and every instinct I possess tells me he likes that.

Answer him, Sam. Be honest.

"Yes," I say. "I like the idea of that."

As soon as the words leave my mouth, he gathers me up, carries me up the stairs and into his bedroom. He shuts the door softly with his foot and sets me down. I glance around his massive bedroom, my gaze landing on his king-size bed. My legs tremble beneath me, my body so worked up it's hard to focus. Am I really doing this?

Before I can second-guess myself or change my mind, his lips are on mine, his tongue invading and conquering my mouth, until I'm a quivering mess of need. He breaks the kiss and we're both breathless. As I stand there trying to fill my lungs, he puts his hands on my shoulders, and guides me to my knees.

"Fuck yeah, just like that," he says as I instinctively put my hands on my thighs and lift my head, my mouth opened slightly. "You want my cock, Sam? You want me to feed it to you?"

I gulp, excited by the way he talks to me. "Yes," I whimper.

"Take your top off, show me your pretty tits, and I'll give you what you want."

I unbutton my blouse, shrug it from my shoulders. As it falls from my body, my skin comes alive, little lightning strikes zapping all my erogenous zones as his gaze moves over my near nakedness. I don't think I've ever been so turned on in my entire life.

He rips open his pants. "Keep going," he demands in a firm voice that teases my clit.

I reach behind my back, unhook my bra and let it fall

from my body. The hiss that escapes his mouth fills me with a new kind of need, and bolsters my confidence.

He pulls out his cock, and I open my mouth for him, letting him know I'm ready. He grips my hair, wraps it around his hand and inches his cock into my mouth, offering me only his crown. I try to move, to take more of him in, but he controls the depth by tugging on my hair. I whimper, my body burning up, on fire as he takes charge.

"Such a greedy girl," he says, and gives me more, until he hits the back of my throat, and I choke a little. He pulls out, but I don't want that. I want it rough and hard. I *want* to choke. I know I shouldn't want that. Nice girls don't want it dirty, right?

As I fight that war, I glance up at him, and he's looking at me very carefully, like he can sense my struggle.

"Rub your tits for me, Sam. Pinch your nipples. Hard."

Oh, God.

I do as he commands and pinch my nipples, pulling and stretching them until pain bleeds into pleasure. His hips jerk forward and he hits the back of my throat again. I moan with want, and he pumps into me a few more times before tugging me to my feet.

His hands slide down my back, and he slaps my ass through my jeans. I revel in the sting his big palm leaves, wanting nothing more than to remove my pants and have him redden my ass.

"I need to taste you," he says. "I want my mouth right here." He pushes a hand between my legs, and rubs my sex through my pants. He puts his nose to my neck and inhales. "You smell like vanilla. Will you taste like it, too?"

Before I can answer, he drops to his knees, using deft fingers to open my pants and slide them to my feet. I hold his shoulders as I step out of them, standing before him in nothing but my thong.

"Nice," he says and stands back up. He circles me, and I quake as he grips the front of my thong, giving it a little tug. It tightens over my inflamed clit, and I whimper in bliss.

"Yes," I murmur, and let my head roll, my hair falling down my back.

Touch me.

"Tell me what you expected?" he says, taking me by surprise.

"What?"

"Earlier today. You said I wasn't what you expected."

"You're better than anything I expected," I admit honestly.

He chuckles. "So are you." He tugs on my panties again, and I nearly climax. "Did you think about me after I left?"

"Yes," I say.

"What did you think about?"

"I...I..." Oh, God, what am I supposed to say?

"Sam, don't you know the rules?"

"Rules?"

"Every truth gets you closer to what you want," he says, and slides a finger over my sopping-wet sex.

"Zander, please..."

"Answer the question, and I'll give you what you want."

"I thought about you. Thought about touching you, maybe kissing you."

His hands go to my breasts and he squeezes them. I let loose a moan. "What else?"

I take deep breaths, not sure I can do this. What if, like the time with my ex, I go too far and it freaks him out.

What if it doesn't?

"What else," he demands, his voice dropping an octave.

"I...I thought about going to my knees for you."

"Fuck," he curses under his breath, and slides a thick finger into me. My hips canter forward, taking him all in and wanting more. He strokes the hot bundle of nerves inside me, and I'm so goddamn close it's a struggle to breathe.

"And..."

Since I'm too far gone to back down now, I take a chance and say, "And then I thought about you having your way with me, bending me over and driving your cock into me so hard and deep, that I'd still be able to feel you next week."

"Motherfucker," he says, and none too gently shoves a second finger into me. He sinks to his knees and closes his mouth over my sex as he fucks me hard with his fingers, and draws my cleft between his teeth.

"Yes!" I cry out, and grip his shoulders, the dual pleasure taking me higher and higher, to a place where the air is thin and nothing exists but this man and what he's doing to me. He changes the pace and tempo, finger-fucking me with hard, blunt strokes. As he indulges, eats at me, pleasure hits between my legs. My knees weaken, and I lean forward to ride out the delicious, pulsing waves of ecstasy.

"That's it," he murmurs from deep between my legs. "Come all over me, Sam."

I do as he says and completely let go, revel in the way this man talks to me, forces me to say what I really want. I come and come and come some more, and when my body finally stops spasming, he climbs to his feet and presses his lips to mine.

I taste myself on his tongue, and as he kisses me, he murmurs, "Vanilla. Now *that's* the best thing I've ever put in my mouth."

My entire body heats up again, because this sex is anything but vanilla. This sex, well...it's what I crave—what I swore I'd never ask for again.

He slides a finger into me, and I clench around him. He chuckles softly as I yelp. "I'm going to put my cock in here," he says. He's not asking, he's telling, and a cry of pleasure catches in my throat. "I'm going to fuck you, Sam. I want your hot cum on my cock."

He kicks off his pants, removes his shirt, and guides me to his bed. The back of my knees hit, and he turns me until I'm facing the other way. One hand goes to the back of my neck, and he tucks the other around my stomach. With a tug, he bends me at the waist and guides me down, until my breasts are pressed against his mattress. My ass is in the air to him, and while I should feel self-conscious, I don't. Even though I've only ever had nice-girl sex with my ex, and have always felt ashamed of my wants, in this moment, the only thing running through my brain is his fat cock, and how much I want it inside me.

"Please fuck me," I murmur.

"I will," he says, his calloused hands running over my ass. "Once you tell me another truth."

"What?" I cry out, willing to admit anything so I can get him inside me. He slaps my ass, and I wiggle as he rubs the sting left behind.

"Why did you come here tonight?"

"To bring you pie."

He slaps me again. "Why did you come here tonight?"

"I...I wanted to see you."

"Why did you want to see me?"

Oh, God, just fuck me already.

"I wanted you to...do things to me."

"Like fuck you?"

"Yes," I say shamelessly.

"But you don't normally do things like this, do you?"

This man can read me like an open book. "No," I admit.

His nightstand opens and foil crinkles in my ear. Yes!

He sheathes himself and pushes his crown into me, and I grip the bed sheets, curl them in my hand as his fat head stretches my tight opening.

"Then why tonight? Why me?"

"I'm not sure, to be honest."

"Not a good enough answer," he says—and starts to inch out.

"No, wait!" I cry out. "I just...there's something about you. Something confident and dominant and I...I thought you could give me what I wanted."

"And what do you want, Sam?" he asks as he pushes back inside. My breathing changes, grows harsher, and I take deep, gulping breaths as he grips my hips for leverage, his fingers biting into my flesh hard enough to bruise me.

"Dirty sex. Filthy sex," I finally admit.

In one fast thrust, he shoves his cock into me, hitting places so deep, I nearly black out from the pleasure.

"Ohmigod, yes, just like that," I say. He pulls out and drives back in again, hard, punishing strokes that push the air from my lungs and shut down my brain until all I can see is stars. I whimper, wiggle and push back against his thrusts, and his fingers dig into my skin harder.

"The good girl wanted to play with the bad boy," he says. "But you're not really a good girl, are you, Sam?"

"No," I say.

He leans over me, and his balls slap against my body as he pounds against my sex. My body burns from the inside out and, unable to fight it any longer, I give in to the pleasure. I come all over his cock, and it drips down my thighs.

"You are so fucking hot," he murmurs, and slams home. He stands back up, and I glance at him over my shoulders. His eyes are closed and each forceful thrust is for him now. I squeeze my muscles, and a growl catches in his throat as his hips curl into me. I've never seen a sexier sight. Except next time, I want to watch his cock slide in and out of me.

Next time?

Oh, God, there can't be a next time. There probably

shouldn't have been a first time.

"Sam," he murmurs, and his body goes still as he comes inside me. His cock thickens, and the pulses against my tight walls feels glorious.

When he finally stops spasming, he pulls out of me, and in that instant, as reality comes creeping in and I realize that my ass is in the air to him, unease moves through my blood. I swallow against a tight throat, and my mind quickly revisits all the things I said to him, all the things I admitted.

Oh, God.

He turns to discard the condom, and I stand up, gather my clothes from the floor and dart into the en suite bathroom. I take a look at myself in the mirror, the pink flush on my cheeks, the messy state of my hair.

I use tissue to wipe myself down, then hurry into my clothes. I stand there for a minute longer, embarrassed by my needs. Good girls don't fuck like that, right? Lord, I come from a religious family. My father is a minister, for goodness sakes.

A knock comes on the door. "Sam, are you alright?"

I gulp. "Yes," say quickly. "Just getting a drink." I turn the tap on and let it run as I work to pull myself together. One breath, two, three.

I open the door and find Zander standing there in nothing but his jeans. His brow is furrowed, and there is a concerned look on his face as his gaze moves over me. "Hey," he says softly, his fingers grazing mine.

"I should go."

He reaches for my hand and holds me in place. "Did I do something wrong?" he asks.

Wrong? Oh, God no. He did nothing wrong. In fact, he did everything right, and that's the problem, because I shouldn't want my sex to be rough and dirty.

But I do...oh, how I do.

5

ZANDER

It's been a whole week since Sam ran from my bedroom like she was being chased by the big bad wolf himself. I spent the last seven days trying to figure out what the hell went wrong.

Personally, I like my sex hot and dirty. I like to take charge, and the second I touched her, used my words to torment and tease her body as I controlled our play, it sealed my suspicions that her likes coincided with mine. Isn't that why she came to me? She sensed I was the guy who could give her what she craved?

If so, then why the hell did she run out on me after the best fucking sex of my life? With the way she came in my mouth, and all over my cock, it's clear it was good for her, too. She's not a girl who sleeps around, that much is obvious, and she admitted that to me. Was she embarrassed by her wants and needs? It's the only thing I can figure, and if that's the case, I need to get her in my bed again, show her it's okay to unleash between the sheets and take what you need.

Okay, if I'm being totally honest here, that's not the only reason I want her in my bed again. Sex with the sweet speech pathologist blew my fucking mind. I'm not sure if it's because it's been so long since I've been with a woman, or we really just connected in an intense physical way. Either way, I want her again.

My heart pounds a little harder in my chest as I park my car on the curb outside her house. I have no idea what to expect when we enter, considering she hasn't responded to any of my messages. I called her place a couple times, even sent an email through her website, but no reply.

"Hey kiddo," I say and glance at Daisy in my rearview mirror. "Are you exited to play with Sam again?" She nods her head and unbuckles as I climb from the car.

"I like Sam, Daddy."

'Tham'.

"She likes you, too."

She smiles at me and I scoop her up. As we walk along the driveway, the front door opens and out comes a mother and her son. Sam's eyes stray to mine, and her lids flutter rapidly. She turns her attention back to the young mother, and I listen as they schedule their next appointment. I nod to the woman, who is looking at me with recognition, and her son as they pass us on the sidewalk, and Sam steps from her house, her door gliding closed behind her. It takes my mind back to the day I fixed it, to the night she showed up with pie.

"Hi Daisy," she says, and Daisy wiggles from my arms. I set her down and Sam takes her hands. "Want to go play with Mr. Giggles?" Daisy chuckles and Sam casts a quick glance my way as she opens the door. I follow her and Daisy down the hallway, and wait outside the office as Daisy goes in search of the stuffed bear. For a second I think Sam is going to close the office door on me, but then she steps into the hall.

"Zander," she begins, her voice breathless, like she'd been running up a set of stairs—like she was sprawled on my bed, letting me do dirty things to her. "About last week."

"What about it?" I ask.

"It probably shouldn't have happened—"

"It did happen, and we can't ignore that," I say.

She glances over her shoulder to check on Daisy, then tugs on the door, leaving it open a small crack, just enough to see and hear her. "It was a mistake," she says, so quietly I have to strain to hear her.

"A mistake?"

"I probably shouldn't even be working with Daisy, not after...what we did."

What we did?

Jesus, after the hot sex we had, she can't even bring herself to say the words.

She continues with, "But then I thought about it and decided it wasn't fair to her. I'd like to finish what I started last week with her, but you and I..."

"Were a mistake." I say it for her after her words fall off, and she nods. I narrow my eyes, search her face. "Is that what this really is, Sam?"

She fiddles with the buttons on her blouse. "What do you mean?"

"We had sex. Great sex. But it's over because Daisy is your client."

"Yes, exactly. It's a conflict of interest. And..."

"And what?"

"Don't take this the wrong way, but I'm not looking for any type of relationship, Zander. I'm trying to get my business of the ground."

"I'm not looking for more either, Sam. I have a child to take care of, and a hockey career that takes me on the road. We had fun. Nothing wrong with that, and nothing wrong with us wanting to have a bit more fun."

"I just...can't."

"Okay, fine," I say, not about to push this. No means no,

and I respect that. "But just remember, you were the one who came to me, and you should probably spend some time thinking about the real reason you ran away so fast." Her eyes go wide, and she takes a step back. "I'll be outside. I need air. Please bring Daisy to me when you're done."

With that, I walk back down the hall and leave the same way I came in. I put my hand on the wooden handrail as I descend the steps and it wobbles beneath my palm.

Dammit. It could let go anytime, and if Daisy or any other child were holding on to it, they'd topple over onto the concrete walkway right along with it.

Worried about the safety of Sam's clients, and needing something to occupy my hands and mind, I go to my trunk and open it. I glance at the toolbox that's been sitting there for years, since I helped Jonah do a few repairs on the daycare space Quinn rented. I grab a hammer and a few nails and make my way back to the steps. I pound the nails in, and once I'm sure it's secure, I shove my tools back in my trunk. I plunk down on the steps and glance at my watch.

Maybe bringing Daisy back here wasn't such a great idea. Seeing Sam again is fucking with me in strange ways. In the end though, she's probably right. We shouldn't have slept together. She's working with Daisy, and there is a relationship there built on trust. But goddammit, that's not stopping me from wanting her physically again.

Still, I can't help but think there is more to this, a deeper underlying reason for why she ran away. Is it possible that I'm right about her being ashamed of her needs?

I brace my elbows on my knees, then grab my phone from my pocket. Fuck, I haven't been out in ages. Maybe it's time I hit the bar and found myself a hot puck bunny—someone to help take my mind off Sam and our explosive sex. I shoot Jonah a text.

Want to grab a beer tonight?

I wait a moment and his response comes in. *Carlo's place?*

Carlo's is a bar where I've spent many nights getting drunk and hanging out with friends. Of course, that all stopped after Daisy, but goddammit, I need something to clear my head tonight.

Sounds good.

I pull up my contacts and call Daisy's nanny. She's our full time nanny during hockey season, but she's elderly and lives alone and really enjoys spending time at my place. "Hey Celeste, Zander here."

"Zander, how are you?"

A child on a three-wheel bike and his mother walk by on the sidewalk, and the mother glances at me. Her eyes go wide when recognition hits. I smile and wave to her, and she hesitates for a second. She reaches for her phone, no doubt to ask for a picture with her, but her son on his tricycle races down the sidewalk, and she bolts after him.

"Things are good. I was wondering if you were free tonight?"

"I would love to see Daisy and sit for you," she says.

"I'm sure she'd love to see you, too, and I really appreciate you always making time for us."

"I'll come by right after dinner."

"You good to stay over?"

"Of course," she says and chuckles—a knowing chuckle. "It's about time you got out more, Zander."

I cringe, in no way wanting to talk about my sex life with the nanny. "Bye for now," I say and shove the phone back into my pocket. I sit there until the screen door opens, and Daisy and Sam walk out to meet me.

"Daddy, daddy," Daisy begins. "Sam and I sang the alligator song!"

I grin at that, and put my hand on the fixed rail. I lift my attention to Sam, wanting to keep things professional, but when I do—and notice the way her eyes have strayed to my hand as I grip the rail—it's all I can do not to press my mouth to hers and kiss her like I've been fantasizing about all fucking week.

"You...you fixed the rail?" she asks.

"It was a hazard," I say. "I didn't want anyone to fall and get hurt."

"That's very kind of you." Her gaze goes to mine. "Can I repay you?"

As soon as the words leave her mouth, a groan I have no control over crawls out of my throat. Sam's cheeks flush, and I have no doubt her thoughts are running in the same directions as mine. But now is not the time to be thinking about my wants, not when Daisy is staring up at me.

"Daddy, are you okay?" Daisy asks. I reach down and scoop her up. "You sound funny."

"I'm perfectly fine," I say as she cups my cheeks to give me fish lips. She giggles. "How about some ice cream?" I slowly turn back to Sam. "I could go for a scoop of vanilla." The pink on Sam's cheeks darken, and I ask, "Same time next week?"

She nods, and her throat makes a strange sound as she swallows. Nervous fingers fiddle with her top button, and I really fucking wish she'd stop doing that.

"Chocolate. Chocolate. Chocolate," Daisy chants as I take her to the car and buckle her in. I catch sight of Sam in my rearview mirror as I swing the vehicle around and head to Sweets, our favorite ice cream shop.

A couple hours later, after settling Daisy in with Celeste, I shower, change and jump in my car to head to Carlo's. I squeeze my vehicle between two trucks and music reaches my ears as I head inside. My eyes adjust to the dark, and I glance around the place in search of Jonah. I find him and Quinn at the pool table.

Dammit, I thought it was just going to be the guys tonight.

Quinn sees me and waves me over. I push through the crowd and gesture to the server for three beer, which seems to be what my sister and best friend are drinking tonight.

"Hey sis," I say and give Quinn a hug.

"About time you got out of the house. I was beginning to think you'd turned into a hermit," she says.

I roll one shoulder. "Daisy keeps me pretty busy. But you know all about that."

"She is a busy girl, but a very happy one."

My heart warms at that. I don't know what I'd do if I didn't have Quinn giving Daisy the motherly support. She needs female influences in her life, otherwise she'll end up a tomboy who swore like a sailor.

Quinn hands me her pool cue, and I put chalk on the end. "We needed a break tonight too," she says. "Scotty is with his grandparents."

I smile. It's so nice that Quinn and Jonah found each other and have the support of his family. After Dad died a couple years ago, Quinn and I are the only two left. Well, of course, our mother could be out there somewhere, but I have no idea where and no interest in seeing her. My mother abandoned her kids, and Daisy's mother abandoned her. No wonder I'm too afraid to bring someone into my child's life. Hurt me, fine; but hurt my daughter and there will be hell to pay.

The waitress brings by the beer and hands them out. I clink mine with Jonah's before taking a long pull, but the toast sends my mind back to last week, when Sam and I made eye contact during out toast...and to what we did afterward.

"I heard from Sam today," Quinn begins as she racks the balls.

At the sound of Sam's name, my entire body stiffens. "Oh,

yeah?" I say, trying to pull off casual and not ask if they talked about me. Fuck, how pathetic would that sound?

"She said Daisy is doing wonderful, and that she thinks she's making progress already."

Goddammit, I hadn't even asked after the last session.

Quinn touches her head. "She's a smart little girl. Like her aunty."

I laugh at that, and some of the tension drains from my body.

"Yeah, she's gets her brains from you."

"And her looks too. Don't forget that."

"Oh, I won't." I run my knuckles over her head, the way she hates, and she pinches my gut. "You won't let me."

She pushes me away. "Anyway, Sam said she brought you a cherry pie."

I eye my sister. "Yeah, she did, to thank me for fixing her door. Apparently, that was your idea."

She shrugs. "She wanted to do something nice for you."

Oh, she definitely did something nice, but you don't need to know about that.

I grunt in response and take a long pull from my bottle.

"I suggested pie. I know cherry is your favorite." She takes a pull from her own bottle.

"Best cherry pie I ever had," I say under my breath.

"She said she might stop by for a game. Lord knows I've been trying to get her out of the house. She's a hermit, like you."

My head spins so fast, I kink my neck. "She's coming here?"

Quinn smirks at me. "Yeah, that girl needs to get some action." She gestures with a nod to Todd, one of the servers. "I thought she might hit it off with Todd."

A strange possessive wave of anger unfurls inside of me, and I work to tamp it down. Sam can date anyone she wants. I have no claim over her, nor do I want one. "Todd, huh?"

"Yeah, what do you think?" Quinn folds her arms and glances across the room.

I turn to see Todd walking the room with a tray of drinks in his hand. "I'm not sure he's her type."

Quinn puckers her lips. "Really? He's a nice guy, and that's what Sam needs."

Oh, that's not what she needs.

"What makes you say that?" I ask, curiosity getting the best of me.

"Her last guy…total jerk." She puckers her lips and frowns.

I want to ask more about him, but think better of it. If she tells me he hurt her, I might want to go hunt him down, and that is all kinds of batshit crazy. Yeah, I have a possessive, protector nature about me. I've always taken care of Quinn, but I only had sex with Sam once. I have no right to butt into her life—or her past relationships.

"I should go," I say and hand my cue back to Quinn.

"What the hell?" Jonah shouts from the other side of the table. "You just got here, bro. Shoot some pool with me. Grab another drink and check out the blonde eyeing you."

I scrub my chin, and glance around at the girls on the prowl. I think about which one I might like to fuck, but can't seem to bring myself to approach any. *Fuck me.*

Just then the door opens, and in walks Sam. Dressed in a pair of tight jeans that hug her sweet curves and a blouse with tiny buttons my fingers itch to rip open, she catalogues the room. Her gaze meets mine, goes wide—and instead of coming our way, she darts down the hall toward the bathroom.

"Was that Sam?" Quinn asks, trying to look around me.

"Yeah," I mutter.

"Where is she going?"

"I don't know," I practically yell at her.

I don't take my eyes off Sam as she disappears down the hall, her sweet ass cradled so nicely in her jeans. I'm not the only guy watching, either. I catch the lewd way some douche bag is staring at her, like a lion about to slaughter the lamb. He sets his beer down and follows behind her.

Oh, fuck no.

"I should go check on her," Quinn says.

I put my hand on her shoulder to still her. "I'll go." With long, determined strides, I cut through the crowd and go down the hall. The douche bag is lingering outside the little girls' room when I arrive, and I lean against the wall and fold my arms over my chest.

His glossy eyes meet mine, and he wobbles a bit. "Wait, aren't you—"

"Yeah, that's me," I say, and gesture toward the door. "And she's mine."

"Oh, shit. I wasn't... I was just going to talk to her, offer to buy her a drink." He holds his hands up, palms out, and stumbles backward a bit. "I didn't know."

"Now you do," I say and gesture to the little boys' room, a suggestion for him to disappear. He shoves the door open and darts inside.

I wait a moment longer, and the girls' room door finally creaks open. Sam sucks in a fast breath when she sees me standing there.

"What...what are you doing, Zander?" She looks up and down the hall, but it's only the two of us.

"Hanging out in the hall and making sure you're safe."

She stands up a bit straighter and squares her shoulders. "I'm a big girl. I can take care of myself."

"And why would you want to do that when I can take care of you?" I ask as I step into her, crowd her with my frame—test her. The heat arcing between our bodies is enough to generate a week's worth of electricity and light up the club in a blackout.

Her breathing changes, and the hunger in her eyes fucks me over. "I told you we can't. I don't want—"

"Tell me you don't want *this*," I say, and grab her hands and put them over her head. I pin her to the wall and put my lips near her ear, all the while gauging her reactions. I won't do anything she doesn't want, and while she's saying one thing, the heat in her eyes tells a different story. And goddammit, I want to help her push past her inhibitions, give her what she wants. "Tell me you don't want me to fuck you right here, where anyone could walk by and see us."

"Oh, God," she says.

"Tell me you don't want my cock inside you again, fucking you so hard you can't even remember your name." Her entire body quivers beneath me and her lips part, an invitation I'm not about to ignore. "How about I take you into that bathroom, and bend you over the sink, and give it to you hot and dirty?"

"Jesus," she murmurs, as I close my mouth over hers, kiss her deeply.

The sound of a bathroom door opening registers in my brain, and while I know she likes it dirty, I'm not about to expose her to anyone. That talk was for stimulation purposes only. I tug her to me, push through the little girls' room door, and lock it behind me.

Once inside, I step back and take in her rapid-fire breathing, the way her chest is expanding and tightening. I want her on her knees, I want that sweet mouth wrapped around my hard cock, but I'm not about to shove her down here, on the bathroom floor in a dingy club. We both might like it rough and dirty, but her well-being is important to me, and the gentleman in me knows where to draw the line.

Later though, when I get her back to her place, she'll go to her knees for me, take me deeper than before.

"Take your pants down, bend over that sink, and show me that hot little pussy of yours."

"Zander," she says, breathlessly.

"Did you think I was asking, Sam?" I open my pants and take my cock into my hand. Her gaze drops, and her eyes go wide as I stroke myself. "You want this?" I ask. Her head nods, and I'm not even sure she realizes she's doing it. "Good, then do as I say, and I'll fuck you like you need to be fucked."

She gulps and steps back. For a second I think she's about to run, deny her needs, but then her hand goes to her jeans. The hiss of the zipper is music to my ears as she opens her pants, and wiggles them down.

"Don't takes them off. Just to your knees." She does as I want and then turns around, bending herself over the sink. I step up to her, loving the way her legs are locked together, her pussy on display, and sink a finger inside her.

6

SAM

What the ever-loving hell am I doing?

Quinn didn't tell me Zander was going to be here tonight. If she had, I never would have come.

But oh, I'm so glad I did.

I move against his invading finger and lift my head, catch the intensity in his gaze as he stares back at me in the mirror. Our eyes lock, hold as I move my hips, take—crave—everything he's willing to give me. There is a part of me that registers the truth here. Zander likes me like this, is encouraging me to unleash with him, but that wanton, dirty part of my mind is at war with the daughter of a minister. Although I can't think about that right now, not when he's fucking me in a public bathroom, and fulfilling one of my many dirty fantasies.

"Did you know my sister was going to set you up with a nice guy tonight, Sam?" he asks, his voice hard, tight, maybe even a little jealous, as he plunges another finger into me.

I swallow and work to find my voice as my pleasure

skyrockets. I grip the sinker harder, and my knuckles turn white as I hang on for the filthiest fuck of my life.

"I had a feeling. She's always trying to set me up," I manage to get out.

"Do you want me to stop fucking you with my fingers so you can go find *Todd*?"

He says *Todd* like it's left a bad taste on his tongue. Speaking of tongues...he's so good with his, and I can't deny I want it on my body again—one part in particular.

"No, I don't want that."

He scissors his fingers inside me, and every last inhibition I have melts away. I moan and give myself over to him.

"You don't really want a nice guy, do you? One who's going to be sweet and vanilla with you?"

I swallow, and his fingers still inside me.

"Answer me."

"No," I blurt out.

"What do you want?"

"I want *you*, Zander. I want a guy who's going to do and say filthy things to me."

"Then why did you run away?"

I tear my gaze away and glance down at the sink, suddenly unable to meet his stare in the mirror. "I shouldn't want this," I answer honestly, a niggle of guilt creeping back in. "It's...wrong."

He cups my chin, lifts it until we're eye to eye in the mirror again. I gulp at the raw need staring back.

"There is *nothing* wrong with what we're doing. You should never be embarrassed by your needs, Sam. Not with me." His finger moves inside me again. His brow furrows, like he's remembering something. "I'm not sure who fucked you up in the past, but you're with *me* now, and seeing you let go and offer yourself up to me so I can fuck you hard is the sexiest thing in the world."

A measure of bliss races through me, his words bolstering my confidence and tamping down the guilt. He plunges his fingers in and out of me, so hard and beautiful, it's almost impossible to think.

"Now tell me this is wrong, and I'll stop."

I shake my head and my hair falls into my face. "No."

Zander grips my long strands, tugs hard until my chin is up again. I moan at the pleasure. "No what?"

"It's not wrong."

With that, he pulls a condom from his pocket and drops to his knees. He grips my thighs with his big hands and tugs, opening my hot sex to him. His warm tongue glides over my damp lips, centers on my clit, hits it with lashing strikes that steals the oxygen from my lungs. I try to move, spread for him, but my legs are bound by my jeans and that comes with its own excitement. He eats at me until I'm quivering, delirious to feel his fat cock stretching me open.

"I want your dick," I say, and he chuckles between my legs. I grin at that, loving that he likes when I talk dirty too.

"Do you now?" he asks and climbs up my body, putting his mouth to my ear.

"Yes."

He shoves his thumb into my mouth. "Show me how you're going to suck it later, when I get you back to your place."

I close my lips around his thumb, and he watches in the mirror. My lids shut and I work his thumb, moaning in bliss, until his cock is pulsing against my backside, clamoring to get into my tight opening. I wiggle, trying to tease him, and he pulls his finger from my mouth.

"Let me suck it now," I say, and don't miss the pleading tone in my voice.

"Not here. I don't want you on this floor," he says and, oddly enough, his consideration fills me with warmth. He likes it dirty, too, but he has standards, cares about my well-being. Damn, a girl could get used to a guy like that.

"I need in here," he says, and shoves his tip into my tight opening. With my legs locked together, I have no idea how he's going to get in, but once he does it's going to be mind-blowing.

He puts a hand around my waist and cradles my stomach. With a little pull, I go lower and brace the side of my face on the edge of the sink. The cool porcelain feels glorious against my hot flesh. Some small working brain cell reminds me Quinn is waiting for me, could possibly come looking for me.

"What if someone comes?" I say, but it turns to a moan as he gives me an inch, and then another, and oh my God the guy has so many glorious inches to give.

"That's the plan, Sam." His voice is deep, tortured, and knowing I can make him sound like that turns me on even more. I rear back, and take more of him, before he's offered it, and he growls and slaps my ass.

"Don't move."

I whimper and want to challenge him, but I'm too afraid he'll stop, so I go perfectly still and let him feed me his cock. I gasp as he seats himself so high, he's against my cervix, and plunging deeper. But I want it harder, I want to ache inside.

"Fuck me, Zander," I cry out. "Fuck me with that beautiful fat cock of yours."

"Jesus," he murmurs, and I blink my eyes, a little shocked at my bluntness, to be honest. I'm not sure what it is about this man, but he can sure bring out the dirty girl in me. He inches almost all the way out and slams in so hard, my back teeth clench.

"Yesss..." I hiss. He does it again and again and again, his balls slapping against my legs and his dick filling me to the hilt. One hand snakes around my body and strokes my swollen clit, and just like that I'm freefalling from the cliff.

I open my mouth to scream his name, but the intense pleasure steals my words. I catch his eye in the mirror, my mouth in the shape of an O, as he continues to pound, drawing out my pleasure. His face contorts, and I love the way he unleashes, not at all embarrassed or ashamed of his needs. He curls into me and throws his head back as he releases high inside me. Once he's drained, he falls over my back, his hot breaths ticking my flesh as we both gasp for air.

He slides a hand between my chin and the sink, pillowing my face, and my pulse leaps at the sweet gesture. He's a wild man in the bedroom, but he's also a really considerate guy. I could get use to that.

No, no, don't go there. This is sex and nothing more, and that's just what you want. Hot, dirty sex with a bad boy.

"You're incredible," he whispers against my skin. He stands and lifts me with him. His hands slide around my body, cup my full breasts through my shirt and give a little squeeze.

"I haven't spent enough time here," he says. "Christ, I never even got you out of your shirt, but no worries. Next time, I'm going to slide my cock right in between them."

I moan. "If you keep that up, we'll never get out of this bathroom."

He chuckles, and the breath of air pushes my hair into my face. He pulls it back and says, "I'm okay with that."

"Quinn must be wondering what happened to us."

He sighs. "Yeah, we should get back."

He disappears into the bathroom stall, comes back with some tissue and wipes me clean. I stand there for a second, just staring at him.

"Sam?" he asks. "You okay?"

"Sure," I say, although I'm not sure I'll ever be okay again. This guy is so incredibly sweet, it's like Cupid's arrow to the heart, but no matter what, I can't—won't—fall for him. Cripes, I'd only end up screwing things up, anyway.

I tug my pants up and check myself in the mirror. "Crap," I say.

"What?"

"I look like I've just has sex in the bathroom."

He steps into me, presses his chest to my back. "You kind of did."

"Yeah, but I don't want the world to know it."

He frowns for a second, then his forehead smooths out. "You're right. Quinn would read more into this."

"We can't let her know or think there's anything between us."

"You're right."

I wave my hand in front of the paper towel until it spits out a brown sheet. I do it a couple more times until I have enough. I run cold water and wet the paper, then put it to my cheeks to wash away the heat from my post-orgasm bliss. Once my skin has returned to its normal color, I pull a comb from my purse to fix my hair and then apply a thick layer of lipstick.

"Beautiful," Zander says.

I turn to face him, and my heart nearly stalls. Honest to God, he's the nicest-looking man I've ever set eyes on, and I can't believe I just has sex with him in the bathroom. Amazing sex.

I want more.

"We should go," I say.

He nods, unlocks the door—and when we exit, we find a lineup of women.

"Oh," some blonde girl says to Zander. "I didn't realize you were in there." The girl shifts her gaze to me and gives me a once-over.

Yeah, okay, I get it. I don't look like her. Bleached blonde and rail thin. I like to have a sandwich or a microwave dinner every now and then. I'm guessing I'm not Zander's regular type, but from the way he just took me in the bathroom, he doesn't seem to have a problem with that. Still, I can't help but wonder about the attraction between us. He said he's not about to bring a woman into Daisy's life. Since I'm not his normal type, maybe he's not worried he's going to fall for me

That thought shouldn't bother me. I mean, I don't want more either.

He puts his hand on the small of my back and guides me to the pool table.

"Sam, what happened to you? I was about to send out a search party," Quinn says and pulls me in for a hug. I hug her back and when we break apart, her head is cocked, her eyes narrowed. "Are you okay?"

"Yeah, I'm fine," I say and rake my hand through my hair.

"We were just discussing Daisy," Zander fibs. "Let's play pairs." He turns his attention to the table, and I don't miss the exchange between him and Jonah. I've met Quinn's husband a time or two in passing but I don't really know him.

"Hey Sam," Quinn begins. "Zander told me you made the best cherry pie he's ever tasted." She crinkles her nose in distaste. "I prefer my cherries fresh. I don't love them cooked."

"I'll take my cherries any way I get them," Zander says, his gaze flashing to mine, and I get the sense we're not really talking about pie or food anymore.

Jonah racks the balls, and he has a smirk on his face like he knows exactly what went down in the bathroom. Oh, God, just thinking about Zander going down is doing the most ridiculous things to my body. It's been over a year since I had sex, and my damn body is letting me know that Zander is the best thing that's ever happened to it.

I step around Quinn, who is watching me carefully, and grab a cue. The guys flip a coin, and Zander breaks the balls.

"We're high," he says to me. He's not wrong. I'm still flying high after that incredible orgasm from minutes ago.

"Wine?" Zander asks as he steps up to me.

"No, I'll have what you're all having."

He gestures the waitress to bring another round, and I accept the bottle.

"Cheers," Zander says, heat in his eyes as we clink bottles.

His throat works as he swallows, and I can't seem to take my eye off his hands, or stop thinking about the way he touched me. Good God, he's turning me into a nymphomaniac. For a second I think about introducing him to my dad, who is a big hockey fan. He'd love that, but I wouldn't want him to get the wrong idea about us.

My turn comes around, and naturally I miss the shot. I never spent much time in pool halls growing up. We play a bit longer, and Zander wins the game for us.

"I wasn't much help," I say, and his hand brushes mine. Little sparks of electricity dance along my nerve endings and settle deep between my legs. Jonah sets the balls up again, and this time the guys play, leaving Quinn and I to chat.

We move back from the table and slide onto the plush stools. "So have you checked out the server, Todd?"

Todd.

I remember the disdain in his voice when Zander mentioned the setup. "I haven't really had a chance," I say. "Besides, I told you. I'm off men and not interested in a relationship. I have a business to concentrate on."

"Oh, come on. You're young and deserve some fun, and who said anything about a relationship? Sex is sex, Sam. A vibrator can only do so much."

Truth. And now I'm pretty sure my vibrator isn't going to cut it anymore.

She waves Todd over, and I inwardly cringe. My gaze shoots to Zander, and I note the way his eyes have gone lethal as the other man approaches. Jonah says something to him, and he tears his gaze away to respond.

"Todd," Quinn says. "This is my friend Sam that I told you about. Sam, Todd is studying to be an audiologist. He works here part time."

I glance up at Todd, with his blond hair and blue eyes. He's tall, like Zander, but he lacks that air of authority, the dominant nature the one they call the Hard Hitter exudes.

Not wanting to be rude, I hold my hand out. "Nice to meet you, Todd. An audiologist. That's impressive."

"So is what you do." He shifts the tray. "What drew you to the field?"

I'm about to give my usual answer, one that has nothing to do with my own speech troubles when younger, but someone from the bar calls out to him.

"Work calls," he says. "Do you mind if I get your number from Quinn? Maybe we can continue this conversation over dinner sometime."

Before I can answer, the bartender calls him again, and he shakes his head. "Talk soon," he says, and disappears.

"Well, what do you think?" Quinn asks, her eyes wide, hopeful. "He's cute, right?"

"He's cute," I say, and let my gaze wander to Zander. Tall, dark...powerful. A fine shiver goes through me. Zander sets his cue aside and walks up to us. His jaw is clenched, hard, and I swear he's going to snap something.

He yawns as Jonah moves in beside Quinn. "I think I'll call it a night. It's been a long week," Zander says.

From the corner of my eye, I catch Jonah about to say something, but he stops when Quinn elbows him in the gut. He lets loose a breath, and I don't miss the silent exchange between the two.

Is Quinn on to us? I'm thinking no, otherwise she wouldn't have introduced me to Todd, right?

"I'm tired too," I say. "I'm going to grab a cab."

"You didn't bring your car?" Quinn asks.

"No, it's in need of repairs and making some clunking sound, so I thought it was better not to take it. Plus, I'm a lightweight," I say, holding up my empty beer bottle. The alcohol has already started to affect me. I can't blame liquid courage on my behavior in the bathroom though. Nope, not even a drop had hit my lips and I was dropping my pants for Zander.

"I can drive you home," Zander says. "It's no problem."

"If you're sure," I say. "I don't want to put you out."

He scrubs his chin, but I can see his grin beneath his hand. We both know when we get to my place, I'm definitely going to put out, over and over again.

7

ZANDER

The night air is warm when we step outside, and I put my hand on the small of her back to guide her to my car. Once there, I press the fob and open the door for her. She slides in, and I circle the vehicle and get in the driver's side.

"I appreciate you driving me home," she says, and buckles in.

"It's not a problem."

"What about Daisy, though?" She sets her purse at her feet and casts me a glance. "You must be anxious to get home to her. Is she with a sitter?"

"She's with her nanny. She's asleep for the night, and safe." I glance at her, note the way her hands are folded on her lap, and she's staring straight ahead, her body stiff. "What?" I ask.

She makes a small noise. "It's none of my business, and Quinn never explained the whole situation, but...what ever happened to Daisy's mother?"

Anger curls through me as I think about Shari. Jaw clenched, I back from my spot and turn onto the road. "Did she tell you how she tried to trap Jonah?"

"She did mention that, but then Daisy ended up being yours."

"Yeah, and I wouldn't change that for the world."

That brings a smile to Sam's face. "You're such a good dad."

"Daisy is the most important thing in the world to me."

"As she should be."

I take a deep breath. I don't normally talk about Shari, but suddenly find myself saying, "After she tried to trap Jonah, and we had a paternity test done, we discovered she was mine. Daisy's mother turned her attention to me. I was serious with someone else at the time, and having none of her tricks. When she figured that out, she took off. Last I heard, she'd hooked up with someone from Washington Warriors."

"What... Ah, it's none of my business," she says.

Knowing exactly what's on her mind, I say, "The girl I was dating wasn't ready for a family, so she took off."

She nods and asks, "Do you think Daisy's mother will ever come back for her daughter?"

I shake my head. "I don't know, Sam. On one hand, I want her to, because both Quinn and I know what it's like to grow up without a mother, and on the other, I don't want just anyone to mother Daisy, you know? I don't want her to come back and then disappear again. It's not fair."

"Life really isn't fair," she says, and her hand slides across the seat and captures mine as I hold on to the gearshift. She gives my hand a little squeeze. "Quinn told me you took care of her growing up. That's nice, Zander."

I laugh. "She might be a pain in my ass most times, but she's my sister. Us Reed kids stick together, no matter what." I flick on my signal and take a right, heading to Andover instead of my home in Cambridge. "She was really there to help me with Daisy, especially after I left to go on the road."

She sighs and sinks back into the chair, stifling a small yawn. "I always wanted siblings."

"Just you?"

I nod. "I think Mom and Dad wanted more kids but it just wasn't in the cards."

"Do you want kids?" I ask.

"I don't think it's in the cards for me, either," she says, and I wonder about that. She works with kids every day. Is amazing with Daisy.

"Why not?" I ask, and she turns from me, looks out the window.

"I'm not interested in a relationship."

Fuck man, some douche bag really hurt her. I don't press, getting the sense that she doesn't want to talk about it. I turn the radio up, and she quietly sings along as we drive to her house. I park on the street, since her driveway is too small to fit two vehicles. I kill the ignition and turn to her, waiting for her to make the next move. She reaches for the door handle and tugs. But before she gets out, she says, "Why don't you come in? I'd like to pay you back for fixing my handrail today."

Sexual tension arcs between us, and my windows fog as we both begin to breathe a little harder. "Did you make me a pie, Sam?"

"No, sorry. I didn't have any canned cherries. I only have fresh."

"My absolute fucking favorite," I say, and jump from the car like it's about to be struck by lightning. I help her from her seat, hit the fob to lock the car and guide her up her narrow walkway. I glance at her vehicle. "Hey, I can get my buddy to take a look at that for your tomorrow."

She shakes her head quickly. "No that's okay."

"He won't rip you off."

"I just...I don't really need it right now. It's summer, and I can take the bus mostly."

I frown at that but say no more as she fishes the key from her pocket to let us in. She swings the door open and I follow her in, shutting and locking it behind us.

She spins to face me. "Coffee?" she asks, and I smile.

"Such a nice girl, with such nice manners," I say.

She blinks up at me, and my pulse leaps as dark lashes fall slowly over even darker eyes. "I forgot to offer last time, I won't forget again."

"What else are you offering, Sam?" I ask as I pull her against me, catch her sweet scent. She melts against me, and I love how responsive she is.

"I don't have any beer, but I do have wine."

"Keep trying?" I ask as I guide her down the hall, stopping at the first door. I open it and find her bedroom. Painted in soft lavender, with a comfy-looking bedspread, the room is warm and soft, like her.

"Um, soda?"

"Nope," I say, and continue down the hall, past the bedroom she uses as an office. I reach what I hope is the bathroom and open the door. Perfect.

"The only thing left is water," she says. "Can I get you some water?"

"Yes. Water is exactly what I'm after." I back her into the bathroom, and her eyes go wide when she realizes what I'm up to. "I want to wash the club from our skin, then I'm going to kiss you all over and put my cock right here," I say, cupping her breasts through her blouse.

My God, we had sex just a couple hours ago, and I need her again already. That should give me pause, but it doesn't. Instead, it has me touching the ridiculously small buttons on her blouse. My fingers are too big to pop them through the holes.

"I don't have the patience for these, Sam," I say, and she chuckles.

Pushing away from me, she reaches for the buttons and works them slowly, vicious tease that she is. I growl.

"You trying to make me crazy?"

She blinks up at me with innocent eyes. "Of course not."

"Stop fucking with me, Sam. You've got three second before I rip that blouse from your body."

She hesitates for a split second, her eyes wide once more. Goddammit, she likes the idea of that. Of course, I shouldn't be surprised. I scrub my face and resist the urge to follow through. Her blouse looks expensive, and I don't want to ruin it on her.

"One."

She works the buttons, sliding them through the tiny holes, her fingers moving faster.

"Two."

"I'm almost done," she says, her voice excited, breathless.

"Three," I say, and step into her just as she shrugs the shirt from her shoulders. I go still when I see her pretty lace bra. I'd been in such a hurry to fuck her tonight, I hadn't bothered to remove her shirt. But I plan to make that up to her gorgeous breasts, with my hands, tongue and aching cock. "Now keep going."

She unbuttons her jeans, and I rip into mine, pulling my cock out. I stroke the long length and her gaze drops, takes in my hand movements.

"You like that?"

She nods, and again I wonder if she even knows she's doing it. "You're going to touch yourself for me, too," I say, my tone making it clear I'm not asking.

"I've never..."

"Then we're going to fix that." I slide my hand around her body, touch her sweet ass, and wonder what other things she's never done but might like to try, because goddammit, I want to do all the things with her. "How long do you think you'll have to treat Daisy?" I ask, and the question takes her by surprise.

"What? Why?"

"Because I want to do so many things with you, Sam," I say, and run my hand between her legs. I brush my thumb over her sensitized clit, and her shoulders curl in as a moan catches in her throat.

"I want that, too."

"So how about this...while you're treating Daisy, I treat you."

"About a month," she says.

"For one month, you're mine. After that, I leave for hockey and things go back to normal. You said you didn't want a relationship, and I'm not looking for that either, so I propose we fuck for the next thirty days. I won't interfere with you growing your business. I know it's your main focus right now. In fact, I'm going to help you around here, help you get the place fixed up and put that door in that you want."

"I can't ask that."

"You're not asking. I'm telling."

"Zander," she murmurs as I slide the glass shower door open. I turn on the water, check the temperature and guide her into the tub.

"I'm also getting your car fixed."

"No," she says.

"If you feel the need to pay for the car and the repairs around your place, then fine, you can pay. But we're trading for pie," I say, and she laughs.

"If you keep eating my pie," she pauses and pokes my gut, "you'll turn into the Pillsbury Doughboy come hockey season."

"Then you're just going to have to help me work off all that pie." I put a finger inside her and she clamps around me. "Now where is this fresh cherry you mentioned earlier?"

"One-track mind much?" she says on a moan.

"You bring that out in me." I reach for the soap, lather my hands and run them all over her gorgeous curves. She moves against me, wiggles her hot little ass against my cock as I cup her breasts and play with her nipples, all under the pretense of washing her. After soaping her completely, I remove the nozzle and run it over her body to wash away the soap. It pools at her feet, and I drop to my knees.

Her hands go to my shoulders. "What are you doing?" she asks, and I chuckle softly.

I open her wet pink lips, revel in the sight of her inflamed clit. "Making sure I clean you properly," I say, and focus the stream on her clit.

"Oh, Jesus, Zander."

She wobbles slightly, and her nails curl into my skin as she holds on. I tap her legs to widen them and lean in for a taste. I lick her from top to bottom, bottom to top, and insert one thick finger into her body.

"Have you ever masturbated with this nozzle, Sam?" I ask, and glance up at her. Her glazed eyes are on me, watching me pleasure her. "Answer me." I push my finger in and out of her.

"Yes," she murmurs, and moves her hips to meet my thrust.

"Why don't you take this and show me how you do it," I say, and hand her the nozzle. She does something to the handle, adjusts the spray, and I chuckle. Oh, yeah, she's done this a time or two. She puts the spray to her clit, and I insert another finger. I brush the bundle of nerves inside as she works the needle-like spray over her beautifully swollen clit. Soft moans crawl from her throat and her eyes slide shut. My God, I've never seen a more beautiful sight. In no time, she begins to quake, her body giving in to the pleasure, and as she trembles, my cock thickens even more.

She moves the spray from her sensitive clit, and I let her ride out the waves.

I give her a slow lick, wanting the taste of her on my tongue. As her breaths come in ragged bursts, I put the nozzle back, wash quickly, and then open the sliding glass door. I help her from the tub, wrap her in a big fluffy towel, tying another around my waist before taking her to her bedroom.

I sit her on her bed, and she shuffles to the side to make room for me. As if reading my mind, she squeezes her beautiful breasts together and beckons me closer with a soft, seductive smile. How is it this girl is still single?

Wait, wait. Shit, don't go there. This isn't about a relationship or getting to know the other person. This is simply about two people enjoying each other physically. But goddammit, I do love watching her open up before me, showcasing her needs instead of hiding them away.

"Are you going to stand there all night or are you going to fuck me?" she asks, and I shake my head. Her gaze drops to my tented towel. "I want your cock in my mouth, Zander. Don't keep me waiting."

I take my cock in my hand and stroke. Pre-cum dribbles from my slit, and she licks her lips and moan.

"You want a taste?"

"Yes."

"Get on your knees." She slides from the bed and kneels before me. "Mouth open, and don't taste until I tell you to."

Her lips part, and I run my crown over her bottom lip, leaving a streak of cum behind. My dick jumps in my hand as she just sits there, my cum dripping from lip.

"Jesus, fuck," I say, and almost shoot a load off then and there. She whimpers, and begging eyes meet mine. "Taste," I say. She slowly rolls her tongue out, and swipes it over her bottom lip. The sexy noises she makes massages my balls and drives me mad with the need to get into her tight core.

"On the bed," I say. "Sit on the edge."

She immediately obliges and as she sits there, she spreads her legs, showing me her hot, wet pinkness. I step into her and run my cock between her breasts, and when she squeezes them around my cock, more pre-cum drips from my slit. I fuck her tits, and with each upward thrust, she opens her mouth, laps at my head.

I grip her hair, move it from her shoulders so I can watch the way she takes me. As I fuck her breasts and mouth, she cups my balls and gives them a little squeeze. My body shakes, and moisture breaks out on my skin as I fight to hold off. I need to come almost as much as I need to hang on. But I can't, not yet. I want to be inside her hot, sweet body when I orgasm.

I fuck her harder, almost slam into her waiting mouth, and the need in her eyes grows deeper. I'm close, so goddamn close, I grind my teeth to keep it together. It's almost more than I can take when she writhes and slides a hand between her legs to touch herself.

"Bend over," I say, a hard, rough demand. Her eyes snap to mine, and I step back, my cock instantly missing the warmth of her tits and mouth. She rolls over. Knees on the floor, she bends over the bed and once again offers me her ass. I drop down behind her, spread her thighs, and shove my cock all the way inside her with a force that pushes the air from her lungs, judging by the way she's taking gasping breaths.

I still inside her. We both like it hot and dirty, but she needs a minute to catch up. "Sam, you good?" I ask.

"Yes. Fuck me, Zander. Please..."

I pull out, slam back into her, and her body opens so nicely for me. I go higher, deeper, and if I could, I'd climb inside her. My balls pound against her, and I cup her ass, massage it. I widen her cheeks, find her puckered opening and run my finger around her rim. She gasps, and in an instant, I know this isn't something she's ever experimented with.

I lightly push my pinky into her, just enough for her to know I'm there. She yelps, but it turns into a moan when I bend over her and brush my finger over her clit.

"My God, yes," she says, the triple pleasure clearly working for her. She comes all over my cock, and her hot juice drips to my balls, soaks me, and I fucking love it. I pound into her, chase my own orgasm as I play with her ass and fuck her like a mad man, seriously unable to get enough.

I push once, twice, and on the third time, I come inside her. Cum jettisons from my cock, and the orgasm is so powerful, so goddamn intense, I lose all focus. I fill her with my seed and fall over her, our warm bodies meshed as one.

Since speech is currently beyond my capabilities, I put my hand on her shoulder, give it a little squeeze to check on her. Jesus, I've never been left speechless before. What is this woman doing to me? I've never wanted anyone more. It must have something to do with her reserve, and the way it melts away beneath my touch. It thrills me that I can do that to her, get her to open up and take—demand—what she wants. It's fucking hot.

She moans to let me know she's good, and we stay in that position until my cock grows flaccid. I pull out of her, go back on my heels—and as my brain comes back to earth, I realize what a colossal mistake I've made.

8

SAM

"Oh Shit."

As I lie on the bed, basking in the pleasure racing through my body, Zander's worried voice cuts through me and reality comes crashing back. I push up on my arms, turn over and find him on his heels, scrubbing his chin. Gorgeous blue eyes brimming with worry seek mine, his brow furrowed.

"What?" I ask, that one word catching in my dry throat. I try to swallow but can't seem to produce any saliva.

"Shit, Sam. I didn't use a condom."

"Oh my God," I say, but the responsibility isn't his alone. Protection falls on both of us.

"I can't believe I forgot." He looks to the door, to the bathroom where we stripped. "I have one in my pants." He pushes to his feet and begins to pace.

"I'm clean," I blurt out.

"I am too," he says. He paces some more, going to the window then to my side of the bed. "To be honest, it's been a while since I've been with anyone."

"Over a year for me," I admit.

"Yeah?"

I reach for him, take his hand. I need him to stop pacing, it's making me anxious. When I'm anxious, my stutter comes back.

"But you're more worried about me getting pregnant, aren't you?"

He casts me a quick look. "I don't want any more surprises," he says. "I used a condom with Daisy's mother, but it broke."

I put my hands on his face. "I'm on the pill, Zander." I open my nightstand and take out the packet. "See? No tricks."

He shakes his head and briefly pinches his eyes shut. "Shit, I didn't mean to imply—"

"I'm on the pill for menstrual cramps. No babies in my future," I say, injecting a lightness into my tone that I don't feel. There is a part of me that would love to have kids, but I suck at relationships, ruin them all, and had given up hope of ever having a family my own.

Or have I? In the back of my mind, I know I can go to a fertility clinic.

He shakes his head. "I didn't mean to suggest you were trying to trick me. You must think I'm a total asshole."

"I don't, and I honestly understand where you're coming from. You've been tricked and hurt, and have had a lot of loss in your life. You don't really know me that well, Zander. I get that you'd be concerned, but I'm not trying to trap the Hard Hitter. I've got a happy little life of my own, and a business to nurture. That's all I want or need."

He lifts those blue eyes to mine and puts a hand on my thigh. "The Hard Hitter?"

I grin at him. "Yeah, I know a thing or two about you." I roll my eyes. "You do have a reputation."

2272132221111111

"Oh, really?" he asks, his mood mellowing. "What do you think you know?"

I swallow, then wince at my scratchy throat. "I need a drink."

He stands. "I'll get you a glass of water."

"I have a better idea." I touch his arm to stop him. "Let's do something fun."

"I'm always up for something fun." He glances down at his cock. "But I might need a minute. I'm not eighteen anymore."

"What are you talking about, you're already getting hard."

"Okay, maybe all I need is thirty seconds."

I laugh and whack him. "Come on." I jump from the bed, pull on a pair of yoga pants, and a T-shirt. Zander stands there and watches me the whole time, his hot gaze locked on my body.

"I prefer you naked," he says.

I glance at his cock, which is full-on hard at this point. While I'd like to go another round, I need more than thirty seconds. "Put some clothes on and meet me back here." I tap my mussed sheets and fix my pillows.

"Look at you telling me what to do. When did you get so bossy?"

"Hey, listen, you can't bring that out in me and then complain about it."

Stepping up to me, he runs his hands along my arms, and he goes serious. "I like that I bring that out in you. You need to be who you need to be." His head dips and, catching me by surprise, he plants a warm kiss on my lips. When he breaks it, I'm a little breathless.

"Ah, okay...I, uh..."

"Lose your train of thought, Sam?" he asks and tucks my wet hair behind my ear.

"Yes, and you don't have to be so proud of yourself for that."

He lets out a big laugh, turns me around and gives me a slap on the ass to set me into motions. I dart to the kitchen, grab a bottle of wine, and two glasses. I get back to the room, and he's standing there tugging on his jeans. My heart gives a little flip as I watch. This is a purely physical relationships, so maybe playing this game with him isn't such a great idea.

He turns and eyes the bottle and glasses. "You trying to get me drunk, have your way with me?"

I hold up the bottle. "I hardly think this will do it? I'm a bit of a lightweight though."

His face goes serious once again. "Just so you know, I'd never take advantage of you if you'd been drinking."

My heart swells. "I know."

"Really, and how do you know that since you really don't know anything about me at all? Other than what my sister told you and that was probably all lies."

I shake the bottle in my hand. "That's what this is for."

"Ah, I get it, you're trying to loosen me up with alcohol."

"Not really." I jump on the bed and sit crossed-legged. Zander stretches out on his side, his body long, hard and lean. It's all I can do to take my eyes off him. I open the bottle, pour some into our glasses and set the rest on my nightstand. "You've played Never Have I Ever before, right?"

He grins. "Yeah." He gestures to my nightstand, where I set the bottle. "But I'd rather play spin the bottle."

"One track mind much?" He laughs. I toy with the rim of my glass, and think. "Okay, I'll go first, and no lies. Never have I ever watched a hockey game."

His eyes go wide, incredulous. "That's blasphemy."

I crinkle my nose and say, "Sorry. Dad watched all the time, along with my cousins and uncles, and I mean, I've glanced at the TV when walking past, but I've never watched."

"Well, we'll be changing that," he says, and since he's done it, he takes a sip from his glass. "Never have I ever parachuted."

My eyes go wide, and I take a drink. "And never do I plan on it," I say.

"We'll see," he says, giving me a mischievous wink.

"Yeah, we will." I take in his sexy grin. "Never have I ever watched a scary movie."

He shakes his head. "Sam, you have a lot of living to do." He salutes me with the glass and takes a drink.

"What's your favorite?" I ask him.

"It's a toss-up between *The Shining* and *Jeepers Creepers*. I watch them every Halloween."

"I watch *Hocus Pocus*."

He slants a look my way. "Isn't that a kids' movie?"

"No," I say defiantly. "And now I'm going to make you watch it with me."

"Only if you watch my favorites with me."

"Probably not going to happen. Your turn."

"Mmm, let's see. Never have I ever been engaged."

I take a sip, and note he's veering into the personal here. "Quinn told you?" I ask.

"Nope. Just had a feeling some douche bag really hurt you."

I think about that for a long moment, and he goes silent waiting for me to elaborate. "You're right about two things. He did hurt me, and he *was* a douche bag."

"Want me to fight him?"

I laugh at that and shake my head. "To be honest, Zander. I'm glad I found out what kind of guy he was before we married." I exhale and think about that. In the end, it was a blessing. I was finding it harder and harder to keep my wants suppressed. Did I really want to be in a marriage where I couldn't be myself?

"What happened?" he asks.

"Let's just put it this way, when it comes to relationships, I'm a screwup. I end up ruining everything."

"You screwed up your engagement?" he asked, surprised by that.

"Something like that." I grab the bottle and put another splash into our glasses.

"Do you still love him?"

"No. I'm not sure I ever did. We worked at the same clinic, had the same interests, and I guess we fit as a couple in the outside world. But we didn't fit everywhere," I say, and then go quiet. Zander does not need to know about my past bedroom experiences.

"I see," he says and nods, and I get the sense that he can see right through me, and knows exactly what I'm talking about.

"Never have I ever had such amazing sex," I blurt out without thinking it through.

I toy with my glass, and wait for him to take a drink. This guy has a reputation, he's been with numerous women who are a lot hotter than me, no doubt. I'm what one would classify as the girl next door, not a drop-dead gorgeous knockout.

He sets his glass on the nightstand, and a little thrill goes through me as the blue in his eyes changes from a sunny afternoon sky, to a thunderstorm brewing nearby. The chemistry between us is insane, really, and not something I've ever experienced before. But eventually that fades, as it will with us, and I'm sure come the end of our month, we'll have gotten this out of our systems.

"Never have I ever sent a naked picture of myself to someone," he says.

I laugh, and don't take a drink. "Well, we'll be changing that."

"You're right, we will." He quickly takes his phone from his back pocket and hands it to me. "Put your contact information in."

I do it quickly and hand his phone back.

"Alright, never have I ever gotten drunk playing this game." We both take a drink and then laugh.

"Never have I ever gone skinny dipping," he says.

"Of course you have," I blurt out.

"How do you know that?"

"I don't, I guess. I just assumed." I angle my head. "Don't you have a pool? I'm sure Quinn said something about you having a big pool."

"I do, and I swim naked all the time," he says, and takes a drink.

"Well, I've never been skinny dipping," I say.

He nods. "Another thing we'll be changing."

I eye him. "I'm beginning to think you're a bad influence on me."

"I believe that's why you came to me, Sam," he says, his tone lower, deeper.

A fine shiver moves through my body at his blatant observation.

"Before you, never have I ever had a one-night stand." I say.

He takes a drink, and nudges my glass until it's at my lips. "You're not having a one-night stand. You're having a one-month stand," he says.

"True enough."

He looks past my shoulders, then zeros in on me, one side of his mouth curling up, making him look so damn adorable. "Never have I ever watched porn."

I hold my glass out and salute him before taking a drink.

"No way," he says.

"I might not be as innocent as I look, Zander," I say.

He laughs at that. "How did I get so lucky?"

"I might be the lucky one here," I admit.

He leans in to me and presses his lips to mine. I melt into him and he takes my wine. He puts our glasses on the nightstand, and pulls me on top of him. He kisses me long and hard and when he breaks it, he pushes my hair off my face and angles his head to see the clock. "I should go. Daisy will have me up in a few hours."

"Okay," I say, missing his warmth before he's even left my bed. Damn, that's not a good thing.

"Next time, I get to pick the game."

I roll my eyes. "I guess I should prepare for spin the bottle."

He smiles at me, but there is a seriousness about him once more. "When can I see you again?"

"Tomorrow night. I'll bring a pie by, and since there are pie rules, I guess I'll have to stay and eat it with you."

"Daisy will be asleep by seven."

"I'll be there five minutes after."

9

ZANDER

As Daisy plays not so quietly with her dollhouse, her favorite song blaring from the television, I load the dishwasher with our breakfast dishes, my mind going to last night—to Sam. A smile tugs at my mouth as I think about the game we played, how fun and easy she is to be around. There is a part of me that thinks my sister is behind us hooking up. Not that I plan to tell her, or give her the wrong idea about us. No. I'm going to play it cool, and when our month is up, and I'm back on the road, this will all be behind me. Walking away will be easy, Right.

Or maybe not.

Just then my phone pings, and I reach for it, expecting it to be one of the guys or my sister. When I see Sam's name come up, my heart beats a little faster. I read her text.

My car is gone and some guy gave me keys to a rental, which is currently in my driveway!

I told you I was getting your car fixed.

Zander...I can take care of my own car.

How are you going to bring me pie tonight, if you don't have wheels?

There is this thing called a bus.

Takes too long. You see, this is all about me. The sooner you get here, the sooner we eat pie.

I plan to pay for the repairs.

With pie, I know. We've already established that.

You're a bully.

And we've established that you like that.

You're impossible.

Another thing you like. TTYL, Sam. 7:05.

Wait. Cherry or apple.

Cherry, Sam. Always cherry.

I watch as three dots appear, but a minute later they disappear. Whatever she was going to say, she decided not to. Perhaps I can get it out of her tonight.

"Daddy, what's funny?" Daisy asks.

"Nothing's funny."

"But you're laughing."

I nod, realizing that I *am* laughing and having a hell of a lot of fun with Sam. I haven't had this kind of fun in...ever. Best enjoy it now while it lasts.

"Ready for the market, kiddo?"

"I want to play with Scotty."

Th-snotty.

Just then my phone rings, and I swipe my finger across the screen. "Hey Quinn," I say. "What's up?"

"Did you get Sam home safely last night?" she asks, and I can hear the smirk in her voice.

"Yeah, I got her home just fine."

"I gave Todd her number, they didn't have time to exchange information last night. You don't think she'll mind, do you?"

I pinch the bridge of my nose. She's fucking with me. I just know it.

"She's your friend. You know her better than I do."

"I suppose. Hey, listen, do you want to bring Daisy by today? I have a few friends coming over to hang out, and they're bringing their kids. I'm sure Daisy would love to hang out and swim with them."

"We're about to hit the market, and I'll bring her by afterward. How is Scotty feeling?"

"Allergies," she says. "The pollen is a nightmare."

"Daisy, do you want to swim with Scotty today?" I ask.

"Yes, Daddy!" she yells, and starts spinning in circles. Will I ever get used to all her energy?

"Pack her pajamas, in case she ends up staying over."

I hesitate for a moment. I love having Daisy here with me...but what if she wakes up and finds Sam here? I can't let her get used to her, let Sam be a part of her life outside the clinical setting. I'm not about to set my child up for heartbreak.

"Yeah, okay," I say. "She'll probably love that."

"That's because Aunty Quinn is a lot of fun."

"Yeah, yeah, whatever. Talk to you later." I slide my finger across the phone to end the call and scoop up Daisy. "Let's get you packed up. Scotty wants to have a sleepover."

"Yay!" she says. We go up to her room, pack her *Paw Patrol* backpack, and hit the market, where I pick up a few things I think Sam might like for breakfast. Yeah, with Daisy sleeping over at her cousin's, I plan to keep Sam with me for the night. I'm not so sure she'll want to do a sleepover, but I'm not opposed to tying her to my bed.

A couple hours later, I park on the road since Quinn and Jonah's driveway is filled with vehicles. I help Daisy from her seat and, backpack in hand, she bolts to the front door without me. Jonah lets her in and she dashes past him.

"Hey Jonah, sounds like you have a house full."

"Which is why I'm getting the hell out of here. A couple

of the guys are in town and later we're going to shoot some pool, knock back a few beers. You in?"

"Ah, actually, I can't make it tonight."

Jonah gives a knowing grin. "Big plans?"

"Plans," is all I say.

He gives me a nudge with his shoulder. "You two make a cute couple."

"Cut it out, Jonah. We're not a couple. We're just fucking," I say crudely. "You of all people know where I'm coming from."

Jonah knows all about my past. He had to work through some abandonment issues with Quinn when they first got together. But it's not me I'm worried about, it's my daughter. I would climb the highest mountains to protect her from getting hurt. What's between Sam and me is temporary, so I'm not about to let Daisy grow close to her.

Jonah puts his hand on my shoulder. "Yeah, okay, bud. Sorry."

I relax. "Who's in town?"

"Rider and Kane, and we're not sure about Jamie yet."

"If they're in town for a bit, hopefully I'll catch up with them later. Maybe we can hit the rink for a game of pickup."

"I'll put it together."

"Zander," Quinn says, as she comes into the foyer. "Are you staying for a bit?"

"Just for a minute," I say, wanting to make sure Daisy is settled and happy before I leave. I follow Quinn and Jonah outside, where there are numerous women and children crowded around the pool. My sister sure has made a good life for herself, and that makes me happy. She deserves it all.

"Zander," a few women say as Quinn pours me a lemonade. I greet them in return, and Daisy comes from the house with her bathing suit all twisted up.

"Come here, kiddo," I say, and fix her suit. I hear a few

awws from the women as I dig into her backpack and pull out her life jacket. Scotty comes stumbling over, having recently learned to walk, and Daisy takes his hand to play with him.

"Did you hear the news?" Quinn asks me.

"News?"

"We're headed to Mexico with Jonah's parents for the long weekend."

"Oh, nice." Jonah grew up with a loving family, and they instantly took Quinn under their wing. Now she has everything I've ever wanted for her.

"We won't be around for the July 4th weekend, so no barbecue. I hate for you and Daisy to be alone, Zander." Over the last couple years, Quinn has become the matriarch of our family, always organizing events, and barbecues with family and friends.

"We'll be fine, Quinn. She loves the parade and fireworks."

"You could always come with us."

I keep my eye on Daisy and Scotty as she leads him to the small children's pool Jonah put in a couple years ago. But there are a couple mothers seated around it, keeping an eye on all the children, so I know she's in good hands here when I leave.

I turn back to my sister. "Mexico in July. I'm thinking no."

She laughs and takes a drink of her lemonade. "You never were one for the heat. Personally, I love it."

"I'm with you, buddy," Jonah says, and Quinn shoots him a look. He holds his hands up and says, "But I'm going, I'm going." He rolls his eyes and looks at me. "Like I have any say."

Jonah is whipped but he totally loves it. He walks over to Quinn and gives her a kiss and she beams up at him. I'm so glad those two found each other.

As I think about that, my thoughts stray to Sam. She said

she ruined everything, and that the failed engagement was her fault. But she gave me enough information to figure out what really happened. They clicked outside the bedroom, but not in it. Did she ask for something he didn't want to give? If so, how the hell is any of that *her* fault?

For a second, I consider asking Quinn what she knows, but think better of it.

"I should get going," I say and climb from my chair. I pull Daisy in for a hug, give her a kiss on the head before leaving. I walk myself down the hall and step out into the sunshine.

A car drives by, the driver slowing to gawk at me as I pass, and I smile and wave. Getting into my car, I drive the short distance home and give my buddy a call to check in on Sam's car. I totally overstepped boundaries there, but I'm not going to have her busing, or driving a vehicle that isn't safe. I take care of those in my life, and since she's currently in it, I'll damn well take care of her, too.

Jake picks up on the second ring. "Hey Zander," he says.

"Thanks for getting the car in on such short notice, I appreciate it."

Something clangs in the background, and Jake shouts to someone, then he's back on the phone with me. "No problem. It's the tie rod end. We'll have it fixed in no time."

"Anything else?"

"Spark plugs could stand to be changed, and she's due for an oil change."

"Okay, go ahead and do all those things. Bill me."

"I'm on it."

I end the call and glance around my place. Celeste did a lot of straightening up last night, and I make a mental note to give her a good bonus. I walk through the house, and it's so quiet I can't stand it. I used to love my solitude, but now being alone feels…lonely. I love that Quinn fills her place with friends and family, but it's not really something I've done.

Is Daisy missing out?

I mull that over as I make my way to the shower. What my daughter needs is a mother, one who will love her and care for her and never leave.

I scoff as I shed my clothes and turn on the spray. Do women like that even exist? Maybe they do, but from what I've experienced, they don't exist in *my* world.

Is Sam the kind of girl to stick around? Through thick and thin, better and worse?

Even if she *was* the staying type, we have no future; she's off relationships and insists she eventually screws everything up. Not that I'm looking for more from Sam.

I'm not, and those kinds of thoughts shouldn't be running around my head. We have an arrangement, nothing more, and that's the way we both want it. Everything is going to work out just fine.

10

SAM

With a warm pie on the passenger seat beside me, I drive toward Zander's place, enjoying the sleek new rental car he arranged for me. I plan to pay him back for all of this, that's for sure. As I run my hands over the steering wheel, my phone rings. Since I synched it with the vehicle earlier, I glance at the caller ID, and press the button on the steering wheel to answer the call.

"Hey Mom," I say.

"You sound funny."

"I'm driving."

"Oh, honey, you shouldn't be on the phone when you're driving."

"It's okay, Mom. It's hands-free. You're on speakerphone." When she doesn't say anything, I add, "I'm in a rental car. Mine is in the shop."

"You should have told your father. He would have lent you his truck."

God, the thought of driving Dad's old beater truck from the twentieth century does not sound appealing. Then again, I drove it back and forth to school when the weather was bad. Beggars can't be choosers and all, even if I can barely reach the pedals. We certainly don't come from a lot, and appreciate all we have.

My brain pauses at that thought. What would my folks think of the sports car I'm in, or the mansion I'm driving to?

"I'm calling about the fourth. You can still make it, right?"

Damn, I've been so preoccupied with work, not to mention Zander, I forgot all about the annual family BBQ.

"Sure, yeah, I'll be there." As soon as the words leave my mouth, a knot forms in my stomach. While I love all my uncles, aunts and cousins, sometimes they can be loud, obnoxious, and...nosey. I am so tired of telling them I'm happy being single, that I don't need a man in my life.

I laugh, but it comes out as a snort. I can just imagine the looks on their faces if I showed up with Zander. They'd be all over him like flies to honey. His presence would certainly take the attention off me, and maybe I could enjoy the BBQ and fireworks in peace.

But I'm not about to ask Zander. That's overstepping what we have here. But that does remind me of the text I received from Todd earlier today that I haven't responded to. He seems nice enough; maybe a little too nice. I could always ask *him* to the BBQ, but I wouldn't want to give him the wrong idea. I'm not interested in a relationship with him, so best not to respond at all. Although I don't want to be rude.

I make a mental note to talk to Quinn, ask how best to handle the situation. She set it up from the goodness of her heart, and I don't want to upset her.

"Honey, are you okay? What was that noise?"

Just me snorting...

"Oh, nothing. Just street noise," I fib, not about to share my innermost thoughts with her over the phone. Or at all.

"Will you be bringing anyone to the barbeque?" Mom asks, and I roll my eyes so hard, I nearly give myself a headache. I guess I knew she was going to ask sooner or later. Any second now I expect her to bring up children, and how she and Dad aren't getting any younger, and are still waiting.

"No, but I *will* bring Dad's favorite ribs," I say.

"Okay, dear. I believe Marion said something about bringing her nephew Caleb. You remember Caleb, don't you?"

How could I forget him? Since my fiancé left me, both Mom and her best friend Marion have been trying to set me up with Caleb, the mortician. No thank you.

Dammit, I really should bring someone with me to end their meddling.

"I remember Caleb," I say.

"Oh, good," she says, her voice full of enthusiasm. "We'll see you Saturday."

"Bye, Mom, love you." With that, I end the call and practically bang my head against the steering wheel. I take a turn, and push all thoughts of the upcoming festivities—and the mortician—from my brain.

In the distance, I spot Zander's house. The outside lights are on, illuminating a path from the driveway to the front door, and I get a little warm inside to think he left them on for me. It's been a long time since anyone has been eager to see me, or quite so considerate.

I pull into his driveway, kill the ignition, and adjust the tea towel beneath the pie before I scoop it up. Stepping from the car, I make my way up the long walkway. It's so weird that I have butterflies in my stomach. I've been with him a few times already, yet for some strange reason, tonight I'm all jittery inside.

The door opens as I approach, and I nearly drop the pie when he leans against the doorjamb, looking hotter than hot dressed in his low-slung jeans and blue T-shirt that brings out the color of his eyes. Honest to God, he has the nicest eyes

I've ever seen, and I love the way they're watching me now as I approach.

"Hungry?" I ask, and lift the pie.

"Starving." A slow, sexy grin curls up his lips as he looks the length of me. Tonight, I opted for a light summer dress with small buttons lining the front. It's possible I picked it on purpose. I love how rugged, rough and impatient he gets when tiny button are involved. Then again, maybe he won't even take the dress off me. Maybe he'll bend me over his sofa, lift the hem over my hips and ride me hard. I gulp at that image, and work to keep my legs moving.

"Cherry?" he asks.

"Always cherry," I say, using his words from earlier. "It's also nice and warm. I timed it to come out of the oven seconds before I left the house."

I reach him and he takes the pie from me, using the tea towel beneath it to prevent a burn. Not that it's scalding anymore, it had time to cool down on the drive here. He backs up to let me in, and I lower my voice.

"Is Daisy asleep?"

"She's not here," he says. "She's with her aunt for the night." A storm moves into his eyes. "We have the whole place to ourselves. We can do whatever we like. Make as much, or as little, noise as we want."

"Oh," I say, and my body practically vibrates at the innuendos. I'm about to turn to head to the kitchen when he snakes his arm around my waist and hauls me to him. His lips instantly find mine, and he kisses me with raw hunger. His tongue slides into my mouth, and I taste minty toothpaste.

He breaks the kiss, and I'm practically trembling. He runs the backs of his knuckles over my warm cheek. "I cooked for you. I hope you're hungry."

Two thoughts hit at the same time. One, I think back to

the microwave meal I had many hours ago, and two, he cooked for me.

He cooked for me?

"I'm hungry," I say. This guy might be tough, rugged and hard, but underneath it all, he's kind and sensitive. I knew that from the first time I saw him with his daughter. There are many layers to this man, that's for sure.

"Good, because we can't live on pie alone," he teases, and gives my ass a slap to set me in motion. I head to the kitchen and catch a whiff of something on the grill outside. "I thought it would be nice to have an adult dinner, with adult conversation for a change."

"Mmm, what are you making"

"Steak. Wait, you're a meat eater, right?" As soon as the words leave his mouth, an almost bashful look comes over his face, making him look so damn adorable, I can't help but go up on my toes and give him a kiss.

He scrubs the back of his neck after I kiss him. "I'm not sure that came out right," he says, and we both chuckle. "Let me try again. Do you eat beef?"

"I eat beef," I say.

He gestures with a nod to the counter. "Do you want to make us a salad? The steaks are almost done."

"Sure," I say and glance at the supplies laid out for the salad. I expected to come here and get right down to sex. This is kind of...nice. I start washing and chopping the produce, and glance out the kitchen window to catch sight of Zander at the grill. I smile, feeling very comfortable in this house with him. I search his cupboard for a bowl and shake the vinaigrette before pouring it on the leafy salad. Zander pokes his head in through the back door.

"Medium well okay?"

"Perfect, exactly how I like my steak."

"I thought we'd eat out here. It's a nice night. The table is already set. Just bring the salad out when it's done."

I finish mixing the salad and step out into the warm night. I glance at the table, set for two, and warmth moves through me to think he had this all arranged before I showed up. I set the salad down and notice wine chilling in an ice bucket. Then I turn my attention to his big pool. I walk around it, dip my toe in.

"It's warm."

"We can swim later if you want."

"I don't have a suit."

"Even better." I laugh at that, and he says, "I told you last night, when we were playing Never Have I Ever, that we'd be rectifying a few things. You not skinny dipping was one of them. Of course, there are other things, too."

"Oh, such as?"

He pulls the wine from the bucket, pours two glasses and hands me one. "Oh, you'll see."

"Zander," I warn in a soft voice.

"Trust me," he says.

"I don't even know you." I think about that. It's true, I don't really know him, but on some level, I do trust him. I wouldn't have had sex with him if I didn't.

"Have a seat, steaks are ready."

I slide into one of the chairs, and he places the steaks on our plates. "These look amazing," I say. "I hardly ever cook." I divvy up the salad and put the tongs back in the bowl.

"No?"

I put my hands on my lap and wait until Zander is seated. "Most times I pop something into the microwave." Once he's seated, I reach for my knife and fork, and cut off a generous portion of meat. I slide it into my mouth and moan as the flavor bursts on my tongue. "My God, Zander, this is the best thing I've ever put in my mouth," I say.

He angles his head and grins at me. "Is that a fact?"

I chuckle as I think back to the first night I brought him pie—and the fun we had afterward. "Well, maybe the second," I say. "Seriously, though. I didn't know you were such a good cook."

"I did a lot of the cooking growing up," he says, and I don't miss the pain behind those words.

"I'm so sorry your mother walked out on you, Zander." It's no wonder he's not interested in a relationship. He's had a lot of women turn their backs on him. "That must have been so hard."

"We got by."

"And now," I glance around his backyard, "you have a beautiful, happy daughter, and you've really made something of your life. So has Quinn." That brings a smile to his face.

"I'm glad Dad got to meet Daisy."

"I bet he loved her."

"He did." He takes a bite of steak, chews, and goes thoughtful. "You don't want kids?"

"It's not so much that I don't want kids," I admit. "I love kids. Heck, I work with them every day, and I'd love to give my parents grandkids. Lord knows every chance they get, they remind me they want them."

"Then what is it?"

I fork a juicy tomato into my mouth and the juice dribbles down my chin. Zander reaches out and brushes it away with his thumb. As his warmth travels through me, I find myself opening up a bit more.

"It's just that I mess up relationships. I don't know... maybe someday in the future I'll have a child, but I guess I don't really need a man for that."

He arches a brow and looks at me. "You kind of need a man for that."

"Not really. There are clinics that can help out in that department."

He nods. "Truth."

"I mean, a woman doesn't need a man to raise a child, just like you don't need a woman," I say, sounding an awful lot like I'm on the defense. He looks at me, his eyes searching my face. "What?" I ask.

"I think you'd do just fine raising a child alone, Sam. But it's not easy, and it's not so much that I don't need a woman. It's that I don't want just *any* woman to be Daisy's mother. By that, I mean I have to be careful. If there is one thing I've learned, it's that women don't stay."

"Some women stay. My mom and dad are together, and look at Quinn. She's not going anywhere."

I take another bite of steak as he nods slowly. "I know. Let me rephrase that. When it comes to *me*, women don't stay. Now...what's really bothering you tonight?"

I shake my head, wishing he couldn't read me so well. "My mother called when I was on my way here. She reminded me about the big family Fourth of July BBQ."

"You don't want to go?"

"I do, I just don't want to be interrogated. Apparently, it's unheard of for a woman my age to be single."

He chuckles. "Your age?"

"Right? My parents are old fashioned. They were later in life having me, and think that if you're not married by twenty-seven, you're a spinster."

"Spinster?"

"You know, an older, unmarried woman."

"I know what a spinster is, but I hardly think it's fair for anyone to put that label, or any label, on you."

"Well, we both know life isn't fair." I set my fork down and take a sip of wine. "And Caleb is going to be there," I say, almost under my breath.

Zander sits up a bit straighter, and I don't miss the tightening of his jaw. "Who's Caleb?"

"He's my mother's best friend's nephew." I leave out the
part about him being a mortician. "They've been trying to set
us up since my broken engagement."

"Your ex left you because you weren't compatible in bed,"
he says, a statement, not a question.

I look down at my plate. "I blurted out that I wanted it
rough...and he belittled me, embarrassed me. He said a nice
girl like me shouldn't want that, and there must be something
wrong with me." I swallow the lump in my throat, and look
away, but he reaches across the table and touches my chin,
bringing my gaze back around to his.

"There is *nothing* wrong with you. You're perfect. If he had
trouble giving you what you wanted in bed, then that's on
him, not you. You didn't ruin the relationship, *he* did. But I
have to say, I'm glad he did. Because he wasn't good enough
for you."

My heart crashes harder in my chest. "Thank you," I say.

"I think being called a spinster is preferable to having a
douche bag like that by your side during a family event."

"You're right. I was actually thinking..." I let my words fall
off. *Don't go there, Sam. Don't ask him. That's not what this is about.*

"Thinking what?"

"Just...about bringing someone, to shut them up."

"Do you have someone in mind?"

"Well no, not really. But can you imagine their faces if I
brought you? My father is a huge hockey fan. That would get
them off my back for sure."

"Are you asking me to go, Sam?"

The food in my stomach bounces as I meet his intense
gaze. My brains races for an answer. If I say yes, will he end
this now, tell me I'm taking things in a direction he's not

willing to go? Or will he agree, and simply see it as helping a girl out?

"I...maybe."

"Yes or no?"

I gulp. "Zander, I—"

"Yes or no?"

"Yes," I blurt out.

And he leans back in his chair, putting a measure of distance between us.

He stares at me long and hard, and my chest rises and falls, never having seen him so serious or intense before. I'm about to push my chair out, run back to my car and kicking myself for ruining what we have here because I couldn't keep my mouth shut...again.

"Fine. I'll go."

I swallow. Hard. "You will?"

"Sure." He steeples his fingers. "But there are rules."

My body heats up as things turn sexy. "Of course there are rules. I wouldn't expect anything less from you."

"Then we'll start with you stripping. Right here. Right now."

11

ZANDER

I love the way her cheeks flush and her eyes go wide when I demand things of her. Her fiancé must have been a total asshole if he couldn't give her what she wanted in the bedroom.

She stands and her hands go to her buttons.

I tap my steepled fingers against my chin. "Nice and slow, Sam."

She works those damn small buttons, and I grab my phone from my pocket and add a little music to the mix.

"I've never done a striptease before," she says, her voice low, sexy, her arousal evident by the way her eyes are dilating.

"That's what you get for wearing a dress with ridiculous buttons."

"Oh, this is punishment is it?"

I grin at her and adjust my pants to accommodate my thickening cock. "Not for me."

"Not for me, either," she says, and I love the fucking confidence she's excluding, love that I can help her free herself and understand that there is no wrong where sex is concerned, as long as it's between two consenting adults. If I ever cross paths with her ex...

My hands fist at my sides, but I take a deep breath to tamp down my anger. Now is not the time or place. No, now is the time to put my hands and mouth on this gorgeous woman before me, worship her body the way it was meant to be worshiped.

I stand, and my chair flies backward. Time to get her wet...really, really wet. She removes her dress and stands before me in a sexy lace bra and matching panties. I gaze at her, and she laughs.

"Like what you see?"

"Fuck yeah, I do." I slowly lift my eyes. "The hottest woman on the planet is stripping for me. What's not to like?"

She stiffens at that, her lids fluttering rapidly. "You don't have to say things like that."

"You think I'm feeding you a line, Sam?"

She wiggles her hips and hooks her fingers into the lacy band of her panties. "I saw the way the girls at the club were looking at you the other night. I don't quite measure up."

"How is this for measuring up," I say, and step up to her, push my raging hard-on against her hip. "You're the woman I'm with. The woman I want. Intelligent, beautiful, caring."

She blinks up at me, her gaze hungry, needy, bold as she reaches behind her back and unhooks her bra. Before it slides from her body, I take it in my hand, run the lace through my fingers.

"Perfect for tying you up with," I say, and her entire body quivers.

Her fingers go back to her panties. She turns her back to me, wiggling as she draws then down her legs.

"You keep shaking your ass at me like that, and I just might fuck it."

She gulps. "I've never—"

I know."

She steps from her panties, and I shed my clothes and scoop her up.

"Never have I ever gone skinny dipping," she says, as I walk to the edge of the pool and jump in with her. She yelps, and we go under. When she comes up, she's laughing and pushing her hair from her forehead.

"I'm going to do a lot of first with you, aren't I, Zander?"

I gather her into my arms, put my lips near hers. "If you want to."

"I do." She pushes off me and swims away. "Now what was that you said about tying me up?"

"Tease."

"I believe that's what you like about me."

"I'm going to tie you up, Sam." I'm not asking right now, I'm telling, and the widening of her eyes lets me know how excited she is about that.

"First you have to catch me."

"I can catch you. I don't just skate fast, I swim fast, too." I dunk under the water and surface in front of her. I pull her too me, kiss her deeply. Her hard nipples press against my chest as she writhes against me. I back her up until she's pressed against the wall of the pool, and she slides her legs around my hips. My cock presses against her warm center, eager to get inside.

"Mmm," she moans as my mouth goes to her neck, to kiss the hollow spot that drives her crazy.

I lift her a little, just enough so I can get my mouth on her nipples. I take one between my teeth, and tug until her nails are digging into my back. I let it go, and lick the sting left behind.

"So good," she cries out and rubs herself against me.

Desperate for more, I carry her from the pool and, with water dripping from our bodies, I head into the house and straight to my bedroom. I don't bother shutting or locking the door. I set her down at the foot of the bed, and dash into the bathroom to grab towels to dry us off. I wrap mine around my waist and, beginning with her neck, I run the cotton over her body. She stands there, arms at her sides, legs spread slightly as she lets me take care of her. I run the cotton over her hard nipples, her belly, between her legs, and soft mewling sounds fill the room.

"Now that you're dry, let's get you wet again," I say, and toss the towel away.

"What do you have in mind?" she asks.

I walk to my closet, and come back with four neckties. I wrap them around my hand and tug.

"What exactly do you plan to do with those?"

"On the bed, arms and legs spread," I say.

Her chest rises and falls rapidly as she climbs onto the bed. I growl as she goes to her hands and knees, showing me her sweet ass as she crawls to the middle. She goes to her back and sprawls out, offering me her body.

"Like this?" she asks.

"Exactly like that," I say. I step up to her, wrap one tie around her hand loosely, and secure her to the headboard. I do the same with other hand, and then her ankles. Once I have her how I want her, I stand back and examine my handiwork. "I might never let you go." She wiggles and squirms on the bed, and I must say, I love having her at my mercy like that.

"Zander," she says. "Touch me...please."

I drop my towel and climb between her legs. I lightly pet her clit, and she moves restlessly beneath my touch. I slide a finger into her, find her so goddam wet it blows my mind. "Are you hurting for it, Sam? Hurting for my cock?"

"You know I am," she says, and I reward her with another fingers. I scissor them inside her, finger-fuck her a little harder, and her head rolls from side to side. Her entire body begins to quake but I'm not ready to take her over just yet. I want to play with her some more. I pull out and she groans in protest.

I go back on my heels, take my dick into my hand and rub myself. Her eyes drop, latch onto my cock. She wets her bottom lip, and I chuckle. "You want this?"

Her eyes flash to mine. "Yes."

"Where do you want it?" I ask.

"You're dripping. I want to taste it." I squeeze my cock, and pre-cum spills from my slit. "Put it in my mouth," she says.

I straddle her and move up her body, until my cock is inches from her mouth. I stay like that and continue to rub myself. She opens her mouth, sticks her tongue out and waits for my cum to drip. I spill onto her lips and she licks them clean. The sight of her pink tongue hungrily eating my cum nearly makes me lose my entire load. I shift my body and put my cock into her mouth, until I hit the back of her throat. Her hands grip the ties, and she tugs as she tries to lift herself up, take me deeper.

"Such a greedy girl," I say, and pull out. I run my cock over her lips, and she tries to get me back inside. I push my thumb into her mouth. "You want all my cum in here?"

"Yes!" she cries out as she sucks me.

"What about here," I ask, and reach down to stroke her hot pussy.

"Oh, God, Zander. Please fuck me!"

I go back between her legs and fall over her, pressing hot, open-mouth kisses down her body until I reach her sex. "Such a pretty, pretty cunt," I say, and nudge her clit with my nose, breathing in the sweet vanilla scent of her.

Her hips lift as her body begs for me. Her hands move,

like she's trying to reach her clit, take the pressure off. "What's the matter, Sam?" I ask.

"Zander," she growls. "Please…"

"This sweet little cunt can't get enough of my cock?" I ask, and nibble on her clit as I insert a finger.

"So good," she says, and I eat at her. Her muscles tighten, squeeze around me. Her small tremors letting me know she's close.

I change position, going to my knees, and lift her hips in the air. Her body opens for me, and I press my cock to her opening. In one fast thrust, I seat myself high inside her, and she screams my name.

"You like that?" I ask. I pull out, ram back into her, and she tugs on the ties, her eyes rolling back in her head. I grip her ass for leverage, my fingers biting into her skin hard enough to bruise. I love the idea of having my mark on her tomorrow… next week. "I want your hot cum all over my cock."

"Yesss…" she hisses, and I pound harder, blunt, maddening strokes that steal the oxygen from my lungs. I gasp, and she continues to cry out my name, her tight walls spasming and convulsing around me as she gives in to the pleasure.

Her sweet release singes my cock, and while I want to hang on, I'm past the point of no return. I drive into her, stay high inside and fill her with my seed. I come and come and spasm some more, until I'm depleted, drained, so goddamn satisfied I have no idea how I'll end this in a month—not when it's this fucking good.

"Zander," she murmurs quietly, and I release her arms and legs, collapse on top of her.

"You okay?" I ask, and brush her wet hair from her face. She smiles up at me, and my heart nearly stops.

"That was incredible," she says, and I press my lips to hers for a slow, soft kiss. She moans into my mouth, and I roll to my back to get my body weight off her. I pull her with me, and she rests her head on my chest.

We lay like that in silence and she twirls her finger around my nipple. "That tickles," I say.

She flattens her hand over me, and I place mine on top of hers.

"I wish I would have paid more attention to hockey," she says.

I lift my head and she glances up a me. "Yeah, why?"

"I'd like to see you play."

"A couple of the guys are back in town. We're probably going to hit the rink for a game of pickup. Why don't you come watch?"

"I'd love to."

She gives a lazy stretch beside me, and I'm about to pull the blankets up—

When my doorbell rings.

"What the hell?" I glance at the clock. Who would be at my door this time of night? "I'll be right back," I say to Sam. I go to my closet and tug on a pair of jeans. I turn to catch her stretching out again. "Don't go anywhere," I say.

"Hurry back."

12

SAM

I'm not sure who's at Zander's door, but I hope he gets rid of them quickly and joins me back in bed. I fix the bedding, and breathe in the scent of him on the soft pillowcase. My entire body is warm, relaxed, yet in need of him again. I try not to read too much into that, when I hear voices from downstairs.

I jackknife up, and tug the sheets up to cover myself. I listen harder, sure it's Quinn downstairs. When I hear a child's cry, my heart leaps.

Daisy.

I glance around the room in search of my clothes, but they're nowhere to be found. I'd stripped by the pool, and now I can't get dressed and get out of here.

I slide from the bed and go to Zander's big closet. I'm pretty sure he won't mind me borrowing a few things, so I tug on a button-up shirt and a huge pair of sweats that tie at the waist. I listen at the bedroom door, and when I hear the front door shut, I inch it open.

Zander is talking to Daisy in a soft, soothing voice. I want to yell down to see if she's okay, but it's not wise for Daisy to find me here. This relationship is a secret, and we don't want anyone getting the wrong idea. Then again, how much of a secret is it if he agreed to go to the BBQ with me?

Soft footsteps sound on the stairs, then a door creaks open. I slip from the room, and I'm walking past Daisy's bedroom when Zander's whispered words to his daughter stop me.

"Daisy, sweet girl. I never meant to let you down. I promise from here on out I'll do better. I should have know you were getting sick. If I could be sick for you, or run to the moon and back to make you feel better, I would."

I suck in a fast breath, and that's when Zander calls out to me.

"Sam," he says quietly.

I back up, poke my head into the room. "Hey," I say softly, as he tucks Daisy into her small pink convertible bed that is so adorable.

"Chickenpox," he says quietly.

"Oh no!"

"Quinn bathed her and put calamine on the sores, but Daisy was crying to come home. She likely got them at the daycare."

"Is there anything I can do?"

He shakes his head and tucks in his sleeping daughter. "No. I might have to bath her again in cool water if she wakes up itchy, and Quinn left the lotion for me." He stands and scrubs the back of his neck. "I can't believe I didn't notice the signs."

I cross the room and put my arms around him. "Hey, chickenpox can come on fast."

"She had a small bump on her back. I noticed it when she was in her bathing suit at Quinn's, but I thought it was a bug bite."

"Easy mistake," I say, and lead him from the room. We go

back downstairs and he slumps onto the sofa. He rests his head on the cushions and closes his eyes. As I look at him, it occurs to me that he's always taking care of everyone in his life...but who's taking care of him?

I grab the remote and flick on the TV. I surf the channels until I come across some scary movie.

One eye pops open. "I thought you didn't watch scary movies."

"Never Have I Ever," I say, and walk into his kitchen. I come back with a slice of pie for each us and the half-empty bottle of wine under my arm. I set everything on the coffee table.

"I'll grab the glasses," he says, about to stand.

"No," I say and push him back down. "Tonight, I'm taking care of you." I dart back into the kitchen and come back with glasses. I pour wine into both and hand one to him.

"What did I do to deserve this?" he asks, and hold his glass out for a clink.

I look him in the eyes and we tap glasses. "You're a good dad, Zander."

He takes a sip and lets out a slow sigh. "Sometimes I wonder."

"Daisy is one of the happiest girls I've ever met," I tell him. "She's full of life and love, and compassion." His smile is soft, and he looks off into the distance like he's a million miles away. "All kids get the chickenpox sooner or later. Best she gets it over with now."

"I should have paid more attention to the bump."

I wave a dismissive hand. "Oh please. My mom sent me to school with them. I was complaining of being itchy and she just told me to stop scratching. The nurse sent me home. Mom was mortified, but look at me. It didn't hurt me. I'm somewhat normal."

"Somewhat," he teases, and I whack him.

"Sometimes with the first child, it's easy to miss things," I say. "By the time the second or third comes around, you'll get better at this. You'll see."

He arches a brow. "Second or third?"

"It will happen, Zander. You'll find the right woman one of these days, and want to fill this house with kids."

He doesn't answer me, instead his gaze goes to the TV, to spot the couple sneaking off to find a quiet place to make out.

"Rule number one in horror films," he begins. "Never sneak off to have sex." He makes a slicing motion across his throat. "They're always the first to go."

Some guy with a huge blade sneaks up on the couple making out. I settle in next to Zander, and he puts his arm around me as I put my hand in front of my face and peer at the TV through my spread fingers.

"I'm going to have nightmare for the rest of my life," I say.

He hugs me. "I think you can now officially say you've watched a scary move. I'll find us something else."

"You sure?"

"Yup." He grabs the remote and starts flicking.

I glance at the clock. "Actually, I should probably go. We don't want Daisy waking up to find me here."

He hesitates for a second. "Quinn asked whose sports car was in the driveway."

I cringe. "What did you tell her?"

"I told her a friend was staying over." He looks at me, his eyes the deepest blue I've ever seen them. "I didn't lie, Sam. You *are* a friend."

"Yes, I'm a friend."

"I think she knew it was you though."

"What makes you say that?"

"She had a weird smirk on her face. It was the same smirk she gave me when we were at the club."

"If so, then why did she give my number to Todd?"

He turns to face me. "She told me she gave him your contact information."

"Really? Why?"

"She wanted to know if I thought it was okay. I think Quinn might be fucking with us."

"Todd texted me."

His eyes narrow. "What did he want?"

"A coffee date."

"It's you and me for the next month, Sam. After that..." His words fall off.

"You and me for the next month," I agree, and try not to think about the lump in my throat.

What? Did I expect him to say he didn't want me to date Todd? That he wanted me to be his girl?

Stupid. Stupid. Stupid. He doesn't want that, and neither do I, right?

I take a sip of wine, to hide the disappointment on my face.

"If you want to stay, that would be okay. Daisy knows you, and we could just tell her you're a friend. I mean, I do, after all, plan to bring her to your parents' barbecue."

"That's true."

He goes through the channel until he finds some action flick starring Bruce Willis. "This good?"

"Perfect," I say, and settle against him. As I melt into his warmth, it occurs to me just how perfect this is. Daisy asleep upstairs, Zander's arm around me, making me feel safe and secure. Yeah, a girl could really get used to this.

I watch the movie, and my lids slowly drift shut, but a cry pulls me from my slumber. I blink my eyes open, take a second to orient myself as Zander shuffles beside me.

"What's going on?" I ask.

"Daisy is awake. I need to check on her. She probably needs more medicine."

"Let me help you."

He hesitates for a second, then holds his hand out to me. He helps me from the sofa and I follow him up the stairs. I stand in the hall as he enters Daisy's room.

"Hey kiddo," he says, and my heart squeezes in my chest. He puts his hand to her forehead, and she wraps her arms around.

"Itchy, Daddy," she says.

"Okay, do you want a bath?"

She shakes her head no.

"How about some of this cream Quinn gave us?" Daisy nods, and Zander says. "Do you remember, Sam?"

"I like Sam," Daisy says.

"She's here now. She's going to help me take care of you."

Daisy nods again. "Did she bring Mr. Giggles?"

"Not this time, but maybe next. Do you want to say hi to her?"

She nods, and Zander gesture me in.

Daisy laughs when I enter. "You're wearing Daddy's clothes," she says.

"Isn't that silly," I tease her.

"You're silly!"

I sit on the bed next to her, and Zander crosses the room and comes back with cotton balls. He removes the cap on the lotion, presses the cotton ball to the opening and shakes.

"Want me to help you with your nighty?" I ask, and Daisy lifts her arms. I gently peel it over her head, and Zander dabs her with the lotion.

"I think she's still feverish," he says. "Would you mind grabbing the thermometer, it's in the bathroom."

"Sure." I go in search of the thermometer and find it in the bathroom drawer. Zander puts it in Daisy's ear and presses a button. "Low grade," he says. "How about one of those cherry-flavored chewables?"

"I'm thirsty."

"I'll be right back," he says.

I sit with Daisy, and smooth her hair back as Andi, her guppy, swims in the gurgling tank.

"Scotty didn't want me to go," she says. *Th-snotty.* "But I missed my Daddy."

My heart pinches. "I know. When we don't feel good, we always want to be home in our own beds."

"I like my bed."

"You have a very cool bed. I want a car bed like this."

She laughs. "You're silly. This is too small for you."

"I could fit," I say, and slide in behind her.

She lays down next to me and her fingers go to my hair. She curls the strands around her fingers. "You're wet," she says.

"I went swimming in your pool."

Her eyes slide shut, and her breathing evens out. I let mine go closed with her, and a second later, Zander is calling out to his daughter.

"Daisy," he says. "Can you sit up for a second."

"No, Daddy."

"Just for a second, then we can go back to sleep," I say.

I sit up, and she reluctantly follows. She takes the chewable and cringes as she eats it. Zander gives her a sip of water to wash it down. I gently lay her back down and settle next to her on her pillow. The sound of Zander's throat working fills the room.

Her fingers curl in my hair again, and once more, my eyes drift shut.

When I open them again, I'm no longer in Daisy's bed, and the sun is shining into the room.

13

SAM

I make a quick trip to the bathroom, and step from the master suite to see Zander coming up the stairs with a cup of coffee in hand.

"Morning," he says and hands me the cup of coffee.

"Morning," I say and take a sip. "And thank you."

"I brought you in here last night, after Daisy was sound asleep. You two were pretty cramped in that car bed, and you'd be all twisted up today if I hadn't moved you," he says.

He pushes my hair from her face. It was damp when she fell asleep.

"My hair looks like a bird's nest."

"Have you ever really seen a bird's nest?" he asks.

"I suppose I haven't."

"Well, I have, the twigs are weaved together beautifully, not one out of place. So really, your hair is the opposite of a bird's nest."

"Hey," I say and whack him. Then I remember Daisy and lower my voice. "How is Daisy?"

He stifles a yawn and stretches. "She was up a couple more times through the night. She's sleeping now, and her fever is down. Fever's scare me. When Quinn was young, she would spike high, and I would spend hours cooling her with a cold cloth."

"Always taking care of everyone," I say, and give him a kiss. His stomach takes that moment to grumble. "Have you had anything to eat?" I ask.

"No, I didn't want to bang around downstairs and wake either of my sleeping beauties." Just then, Daisy calls out to her father. "Coming, kiddo," he says, and turns.

"What does Daisy like for breakfast?" I ask.

"I'm not sure she has much of an appetite, but she loves pancakes with blueberries."

I nod. "You go take care of her, and let me take care of breakfast for the three of us."

He arches a brow. "I don't have microwave pancakes, Sam."

I pick up a pillow and throw it at him. "I'm sure I can figure something out."

Chuckling, he goes down the hall, and I fold up the sleeves on the big shirt I'm wearing and head to the kitchen. After searching his cupboards, I come across a boxed mix.

"Perfect," I say. For a second there, I feared I was going to have to make them from scratch. But if I can make a pie from scratch, I can probably figure out pancakes easily enough. I search the fridge for butter, blueberries and syrup, and set them on the counter.

Giggles from upstairs reach my ears, and relief that Daisy is feeling better moves through me. I go to work on the pancakes, and use the blueberries to make happy faces in Daisy's small ones. I make a couple larger ones for the adults. I turn at the sound of footsteps on the stairs—and my heart grows in size when I see Daddy and Daughter enter the kitchen hand in hand. The love between the two fills the room, and my heart.

"Daddy said you were making pancakes," Daisy says. "I want mine with booberries."

I laugh at the way she says blueberries. I plate hers and set them on the table. "Come see." She lets her father's hand go and rubs her eyes as she scurries to the table. A huge smile lights up her sweet face when she sees her breakfast. "Daddy, they have a face!"

"I see," he says, and pours a little syrup on them. His eyes turn to mine, and the smile he gives me makes me want to make Daisy breakfast every day. "Do I have a booberry smiley face, too?"

"No, but I can arrange that for next time."

Daisy eats her breakfast, and Zander darts her a glance before pressing his lips to mine. "Thanks," he whispers, and that's when I note the lines around his eyes.

He didn't get much sleep last night. But it's Sunday morning and I have nothing on my agenda today, so I plan to rectify that.

We all sit at the table and dig into our food. Daisy has dark circles under her eyes, and I suspect that she'll be back in bed shortly.

"Is she going to have to stay home for the next little bit?" I ask.

"Yeah, Quinn said she can't take her to the daycare, even though that's likely where she picked this up."

"How about Scotty, does he have them, too?"

"Not yet, but Quinn suspects he'll start to show signs soon enough."

"Well, at least she has her Daddy here to be with her."

Zander nods and takes a sip of his coffee. His tension reaches out to me, but I don't comment on it, not while Daisy is still at the table.

He pushes to his feet and goes to the fridge. "Orange juice," he asks his daughter, and she nods her tired little head.

He brings her a glass and holds the jug out to me.

"I'm good with just coffee, thanks."

"What repairs are you looking to have done at your place?" he asks, leading the conversation away from him and on to me. For the next few minutes, I tell him what I'd like to do, eventually. When money is no longer an issue. He nods his head thoughtfully and just takes it all in.

"Daddy, I want to watch *Paw Patrol*," Daisy says.

He nods and stands, holding his hand out to her. "First, let's brush your teeth and change your clothes."

"I want to wear jammies," she says.

"You can. Let's just get you a clean pair."

She nods and her dark curls bounce. My heart pounds a little harder as they leave the kitchen hand in hand, the same way they came in. A little tear pricks at my eye and I blink it away.

If I'm being completely truthful with myself, I might want kids, but I'm not so sure I want them on my own. I'm capable of raising a father-less child, but when I see the kind of bond those two have, it makes me realize how much my child would be missing out on. And Daisy might have female influences in her life, but when it comes right down to it, no one can take the place of a mother.

I gather the dinner dishes we left outside last night, and my body responds just remembering what we did after having a nice meal. And it *was* a nice meal. I can't deny that I enjoy Zander's company, he's fun and easy to be around.

I tidy the kitchen and rinse the dishes before putting them in the dishwasher. The TV sounds from the other room, and warm heat moves through me when Zander comes back, presses his body to mine, his mouth at my ear.

"You didn't have to clean up," he says. I turn to face him, and with Daisy nowhere to be found, I go up on my toes and give him a proper good-morning kiss.

"I want you in my bed again," he says.

"It's too risky with Daisy here."

"I know."

"But I do want *you* in your bed again," I say. "You're exhausted, Zander. Let me take care of Daisy for a bit, and you go have a nap."

He shakes his head. "No, she's not your responsibility, she's mine. It's important I spend every minute with her when I'm here."

"I understand, but you're not much good to her when you're a walking zombie."

"I don't know..."

How can I bargain with this stubborn man? "How about this? You're determined to help me around my place, right? And I know you won't take payment. Consider *this* payment. You sleep. I take care of Daisy."

He stifles a yawn.

"I saw that, you know. You can't hide that from me."

He cups my ass and squeezes. "I am tired."

"Then go. I'll watch *Paw Patrol* with Daisy. It's good for me to be up on my kids' shows anyway. It helps me relate."

"Just don't put on the alligator song, you'll have an earworm for the rest of the day."

I chuckle and give him a nudge. "Go. Sleep. Daisy's in good hands, I promise."

"I know she is." He drops another kiss onto my cheek, then goes to talk to Daisy. I dart outside and gather up my dress, bra and underwear, and grab Zander's clothes as well. I wasn't in mine long enough last night for them to be dirty, and they'll do just fine until I can get home and change.

I rush inside as Zander talks to Daisy and tells her I'll be watching her, and hurry to the bathroom to dress. When I emerge, Daisy is nearly asleep on the sofa and Zander is making his way to the stairs.

"Sleep well," I say.

"Thanks, Sam."

He disappears upstairs, and I settle in next to Daisy. Her eyes are practically rolling in her head as sleep pulls at her, but like every other toddler I know, she's fighting it. I reach for the remote and turn the TV down a bit, and surf through my phone as I wait for her to go out.

When her lids finally fall shut, I tuck her in, and lower the volume even more.

I'm about to grab another coffee when a knock comes from the door. I pad over quietly and peek through the peephole before opening it.

When I see Quinn standing there, I go still.

Dammit. Do I let her in? What will she think of me staying overnight? Last night, Zander said he was certain she knew it was me in his house.

A knock comes again, and knowing I can't just leave her out there, I unlock the door and open it.

Her eyes go wide for a second, but she pulls herself together quickly. "How is Daisy?"

I wave my hand toward the sofa. "Sound asleep. Like her daddy."

"Seriously?"

I frown at that. "Yeah. I told him I'd take care of Daisy so he could sleep. He was up numerous times with her last night."

"Wow."

"Wow, what?"

"I'm just surprised is all. He only ever leaves Daisy with me or Celeste. She's Daisy's full-time nanny when Zander is on the road."

"Oh, he probably trusts me with her because I treat her for her lisp. He leaves me with her in the clinic."

"Yeah, that's probably it," she says with a shrug, and looks past my shoulder. "Coffee on?"

"Sure, come on in." We walk quietly to the kitchen. "How's Scotty?"

"No signs of chickenpox yet. He and his daddy are having a Sunday afternoon at that park. I wanted to stop by to see if Zander needed anything, but I can see you have everything under control."

She helps herself to a mug and refills mine. I grab the milk and give us both a splash.

"Sit outside?" she asks.

"Sure," I say, and follow her out, grateful that I also gathered up Zander's clothes earlier and left them in the bathroom.

"Is that your car in the driveway?" she asks as she settles herself at the table.

"Zander arranged for it. He said he had a good mechanic. I'm going to pay him back though," I say, not wanting Quinn to think I'm using her brother in any way.

"He's a good guy."

"He is," I say. "He even agreed to go to my family's annual Fourth of July BBQ."

"Oh, really?" she says with a smirk.

"I was kind of in a bind. As you know, my folks and family are always poking their nose where it doesn't belong. Zander agreed to come to get the heat off me. We'll just pretend we're a couple for a little while and that should have everyone backing off."

"Pretend, huh?"

"Yeah."

"So, Todd," she says. "Has he texted you?"

"He did." I cringe. "I appreciate you trying to set us up, but I'm not really interested. I want to text him back, but I'm not sure what to say."

"Let me take care of that," she says, and nods her head like she has it all under control.

"Really?

"Sure." She gives a casual shrug and takes a sip of coffee. "I set it up, so I'll see to it that he understands you're with someone else now."

Unease takes up residency in my gut, and I twist the hem of my sundress in my fingers. "I'm not really with anyone else," I say. "Zander and I..." What do I say to my friend? *Oh, I'm just fucking your brother.* That sounds a bit crude. "We're just friends."

"Friends who sleep together," she says bluntly, never a girl to pull any punches.

My face burns hot, and it's not from the early morning sun beating down on me. "Well...yes." She gives me a big smile, but I hurry out with, "It's not a relationship or anything. We don't want anyone to get the wrong idea. Neither of us want anything more, Quinn."

She looks at me, big blue eyes that match Zander's and Daisy's moving over my face. She gives me a small smile and says, "Are you sure about that?"

14

ZANDER

It's been a long week, but fortunately Daisy is on the mend and able to make her late Friday appointment with Sam. I hadn't seen her since she left my place last Sunday after my nap, and I have to say the sleep did me good, but I hate that I missed out on time with my two girls.

Two girls.

Well, technically they are. At least, Sam is until she finishes treating Daisy.

Before she left, she'd given me some exercises to do with my daughter, and as we drive through the city, I glance at her in the rearview mirror.

"I like soup," I say.

"I like th-oup," she repeats. I grin at her in the mirror and she grins back.

"I like supper," I say.

"I like th-upper," she repeats.

We go through a few more words, then she loses interest and begins to play with her doll.

"Are we getting ice cream later, Daddy?"

"Of course. We get ice cream after every visit with Sam."

"Can Sam come with us?"

It's easy to see that Daisy likes her. What's not to like? But I can't let Daisy grow too close to her. "She's probably busy."

"I want Sam to come," she says.

"Okay, we'll see," I say, caving in to her. I really should be a stronger disciplinarian, maybe be a bit firmer with my demands, but it's hard for me. I'm home so little with her, and when I'm here, I just want to give her the world. I'm sure if she had a full-time mother, she's be much more consistent. But she doesn't, so we do the best we can.

"We pull up in front of Sam's, and she unbuckles. I help her from the car and as we walk up the pathway, Sam's old car is sitting in the driveway. I paid for her repairs, and I'm happy with the work my mechanic put into it. It's much safer to drive and it gives me comfort to know she's not going to break down somewhere.

She's at the door, and my heart gives a little leap when I see her. Fuck, I missed her. A lot.

I exhale loudly at that revelation and resist the urge to pull her into my arms for a kiss.

"Hey Daisy," she says, her eyes lighting with real pleasure as my daughter races to her. She bends to nip at her nose with the alligator puppet and when she stands again, and her eyes meet mine, electricity arcs between us.

"Come in," she says. A little breathless whisper. I brush my knuckles along hers as I enter and her heat reaches out to me.

"Head to the playroom, Daisy. I'll be right there," Sam says.

Daisy skips down the hall, and I pull Sam to me. "I've missed you," I admit honestly.

"Did you have a hard week?" she asks, teasing me as she rubs her pelvis against mine. I growl in her ear.

"I want to see you, tonight."

"I want that too," she says. "Right now, I have to go work with Daisy."

"I'm going to work on your back deck. I picked up lumber."

"You didn't have to do that."

"Yeah, I wanted to. And pie..."

I laugh at that. "You're not getting tired of my pie?"

"I'll never tire of your pie, Sam."

She grins at me, and I stare at her sweet ass as she goes down the hall and disappears into the office with Daisy. I give myself a second to get my boner under control before I head outside to get to work on her back step. The late-day sun beats down on me, and in no time at all my shirt sticks to my body. I peel it off and toss it aside. I measure the wood, cut it with the circular saw I brought, then pound it into place.

"Hello," a voice says over my pounding.

I glance up to see a woman coming my way. She doesn't look to be much older than Sam.

"Hello," I return.

Her mouth drops, and surprise registers on her face. "You're Zander Reed!" she says, the can of soda in her hand nearly slipping free.

I nod. "Last time I checked."

She glances at the door, then back at me. "I don't understand, what are you doing here?"

"Sam is working with my daughter, Daisy, and I'm helping her with a few things around the house."

Her gaze drops to my bare chest, and she goes silent for a second. I clear my throat, and she lifts her gaze to me. She lifts one leg, puts it on the new bottom step, and her short-shorts ride higher on her thigh. Toying with the low V-neck of her blouse, she holds her can of soda out to me. "Here. You look like you could use a drink."

I get it. I get it really fast. Sam's neighbor wants a piece of the Hard Hitter.

"I'm good, thanks." I'm not interested in her soda, or her anything. Why would I ever want to bed another girl when I have someone like Sam? Someone who is good to both me and my daughter. Someone who sees me as more than the Hard Hitter.

Someone who has no interest in a real relationship.

"Oh, okay," she says, like I've offended her, but she takes a drink and steps closer. "I'm Katrina, Sam's neighbor." She rolls her eyes slightly. "She has so many people coming and going from her place, I have no idea who's a client and who's...not," she says, likes she's privy to information I'm not —and is trying to paint a picture for me, in case my interests went deeper.

"Is that right?"

"The last guy who did work around her house...we'll, let's just say he wasn't a famous hockey player."

A strange burst of jealousy goes through me as I picture Sam with another guy.

I shake that thought off. She's mine for the month, who she's been with before—or who she'll be with after—is none of my business.

Then why do I feel like it is?

The back screen door whines open, and I make a mental note to fix that next. "Zander—" Sam begins. But when she sees her neighbor, she says, "Oh, hi Katrina. I didn't realize you were here. I was just checking with Zander to see if he needed a drink," she says, and hold out a glass of lemonade.

"Thanks," I say, accepting it and taking a sip. "How's it going in there?"

"We're just about finished. Five more minutes."

I wipe my brow with the back of my hand, and Sam hovers in the door like she's reluctant to leave me with her neighbor. Not that I can blame her. She *is* rather blatant, but Sam needs to know it's her and only her I want to be with.

"By the way, Daisy wants to go for ice cream after her session. Why don't you join us?"

"Oh." She straightens a little. "I...I'm not—"

"Sweets has the best chocolate ice cream in the city. Chocolate's your favorite, right?"

She folds her arms and grins at me. "You drive a hard bargain."

"I'll take that as a yes."

"Yes," she says, and my stomach flips, happier about her joining us than I should be.

"I'll let you know when we're done," she says. "Not too much longer."

I glance back at Katrina, who's still scowling at the door, even after Sam disappeared through it. Funny, in the past, I would have gone for a girl like Katrina. Tall, thin, dressed in barely there clothes. But man, after getting a taste of Sam, the sweet girl next door, and sinking my teeth into her curves, I have no idea how I'll go back to the swarm of puck bunnies, ready and willing to fuck any hockey player simply because of his stature.

Maybe I was getting away from that anyway. My last girl-friend wasn't a bunny, and I cared a great deal for her—until she up and ran away because she wasn't ready for a family. In the end, I guess I don't blame her. It's a hard thing to put on any woman.

"You and Sam," she begins, and narrows her eyes like she can't quite believe it. "You're a couple."

"Yeah, we're a couple," I fib, but goddammit, there's a part of me that really wants that.

"How well do you know her?"

"Not well. You?"

"Well enough," she says.

"What's that supposed to mean?"

"I'll let you figure that out." With that, she saunters away, giving an extra shake to her backside. But I'm not interested, so I turn my attention to gathering up my tools.

I reload my trunk, go back inside to splash some water on my face, and tug my shirt back on. I leave the bathroom just as Sam and Daisy come from the office.

"Daddy," Daisy yells. "I love soup!"

My head rears back. "Daisy, I love soup too,' I say, and we both laugh. I glance at Sam.

"We tried some new exercises today and she's making great progress."

My stomach tightens at that. While I'm happy about the progress, it also means that my time with Sam could be up sooner rather than later, and that doesn't sit right with me.

"Ice cream," Daisy yells.

"All set?" I ask Sam.

"Let me grab my purse." She darts to the kitchen, then locks the door behind us. We pile into my car, and we head to Sweets. Daisy sings loudly in the backseat to some song playing on her kids' iPad. I wince and turn to Sam. "She has her father's voice."

Sam laughs and her hand slides across the seat, tangles with mine, and I give hers a little squeeze, loving her with us like this. A short while later, I park, and we walk to Sweets. We all get our ice cream and head to the park. Daisy licks her ice cream and darts to the slide.

"Careful, kiddo," I say, and take seat at the bench to keep an eye on her. Sam settles herself beside me, and every time she pokes her tongue out to take a lick, my dick twitches in my pants.

Needing a distraction—now is certainly not the time to be sporting a hard-on—I engage her in conversation. "I take it you and Katrina aren't friends."

"What makes you say that?

"Daddy look. Daddy look!" Daisy says, as she goes down the small plastic slide, dripping ice cream cone in hand. I wave to her and turn back to Sam.

"She alluded that you had other men helping you fix the place up."

She laughs at that. "Yeah, my sixty-year-old father. Does he qualify as other men?" She shakes her head and continues with, "She's one of the mean girls, Zander. You know, popular in high school, and now queen bee of the neighborhood. I never hung out with girls like her back then, and I don't now, either. I wasn't popular, or..."

"Mean."

"Right."

"I kind of told her we were a couple. I know we're not, and we weren't supposed to say anything, but I didn't like the things she was saying about you."

"What was she saying?" she asks, not at all surprised to hear her neighbor was talking about her. It bothers me that she might be used to that kind of thing. Girls can be so mean, and I want my daughter to grow up strong and with empathy for others. I want her to be like Sam.

"Basically that she knew you 'well enough'." I pause to do air quotes around the words. "But I have no idea what she's talking about. I only know she wasn't being kind."

"I have no idea either."

"Maybe they're threatened by the pretty single girl who moved in."

I laugh at that. "Doubtful."

"Maybe they're worried you're going to steal their husbands. Have a secret, dirty affair."

"That's what I have you for," she says, taking a long lick of her chocolate. "Although it's not much of a secret anymore. Quinn's fully aware of our secret."

"That means everyone knows. She's never been good at secrets."

"Oh well. My mother always said if others were talking about *me*, it meant they were leaving someone else alone."

"That's a good way to think about it. I'll be sure to give Daisy the advice when the time comes."

I wave to Daisy again when she calls out to me and Sam reaches into her purse to grab her ringing phone. She slides her finger across the screen.

"Hey Mom," she says.

I can't hear what her mother is saying to her—I only know by the whitening of Sam's face, something is very terribly wrong.

15

SAM

I jump to my feet and glance at Zander, who's standing up beside me, deep concern etched on his handsome face. He touches my elbow, gives it a little squeeze to let me know he's there for me, and he can't know how much I appreciate that.

I listen to my mother and try not to panic. She's assuring me Dad is okay, but until I see him myself, I won't stop stressing.

I end the call and Zander is waiting for me to talk. "Dad was in a car accident," I blurt out. "He's at General Hospital. Mom is with him but he has to go in to surgery. His arm or shoulder is messed up. I need to go."

"I'll take you," he says without hesitation.

I pause for a second. We're closer to the hospital than to my place, so going back to get my own car will take time I don't want to waste. "Okay, you can drop me off," I say. Ill figure out how to get home later, once I've seen my dad.

"Daisy, time to go," Zander calls out, his voice tight.

I take a step, and my knees go weak.

"Whoa," Zander says, and captures me. I'm obviously

more worked up than I thought.

Daisy comes skipping over, but when she sees me, her face drops. "What's wrong?"

"My father is hurt," I say. "I need to go check on him."

We make our way back to the car, and Zander's knuckles are white on the steering wheel as he moves through late-Friday traffic. We reach the hospital, and I open the door.

"Thanks," I say. "I'll text you later to let you know how he's doing."

Before he can say anything, I close the door and hurry inside. I go to information, find out where my dad is, and take the elevator to the fourth floor. Mom is in the waiting room when I arrive.

"How is he?" I ask.

Mom stands and takes me into her arms. "He's going to be fine, Sam. The air bag deployed but his door crumbled. His arm got twisted up, and he needs surgery to make it right."

The ice cream sours in my stomach, and Mom guides me down into the uncomfortable waiting room chair. "What happened?"

"Some drunk driver ran a red and smashed into your father's car, driver's side."

"Oh my God," I say, the room spinning around me. I can't imagine ever losing my dad. He's been there for me my whole life. What if I'd lost him before ever giving him the grandkids he so desperately wants?

I settle into the chair and grab a magazine, but I can't focus on anything. Beside me, Mom knits on her scarf, and every now and then casts a glance at the television.

After a good hour of sitting, I stand and pace. "Is there anyone we can talk to, ask how things are going?"

"I'll find out for you," a very familiar man's voice says from the doorway.

I turn, and my heart jumps into my throat when I find

Zander standing there.

Without questioning it, I run to him, and he puts his arms around me, squeezing tight. I fight tears and press my face into the crook of his neck. We hold each other for a long time and when he lets me go, I turn to see Mom sitting there, a small smile on her face.

"Mom," I say. "This is Zander Reed."

"I know very well who he is," Mom says.

"Zander, this is my mom, Mary Peters."

"Mary," he says, and walks up to her. "I'm so sorry to hear about the accident. I got here as fast as I could."

"I see that," she says.

Zander turns to me. "I dropped Daisy with Quinn. She sends her love."

"Thanks. Daisy is Zander's daughter," I explain to Mom.

"Oh, you have a daughter, how lovely. We love children. Can't wait for grandkids."

Zander gives me a sidelong glance. "Sam is young. Lots of time for that," he says.

"Mom, Zander and Daisy will be joining us for the BBQ next weekend. If you're still planning on having it."

"Of course we are. A broken arm won't keep your father down."

"Speaking of that, why don't you go have a seat. I'll get us all coffee and see if I can find anything out."

"Thank you," I say, and he brushes his thumb along my cheek before disappearing.

I exhale loudly and sit, staring at the ceiling.

"I believe it's your father's heart we should be worried about," Mom says, and I sit up.

"What's wrong with his heart?"

She chuckles softly. "When the Hard Hitter shows up for the barbeque, your father's going to have a heart attack."

"Oh," I say, and laugh with her.

"How did you two meet?"

"You remember my friend Quinn? Zander is her brother, and his little girl needed some speech therapy. Wait until you meet her, she's adorable."

"Sounds like you really like her."

"I do. Zander is so good with her."

"And where is the child's mother?"

"Not in the picture, sadly."

"Sad indeed."

I lean back again, and think about how hard it must have been for Zander to have his mother walk out without so much as a backward glance. He's been through a lot, which makes me want to take care of him all the more.

He comes back with three cups of coffee and hands them out. He sets a bag with sugar, creamers and stir sticks on the table. "All they could tell me was that he was still in surgery."

I nod, and he takes a seat beside me. Mom continues to knit, making small talk about hockey. Since I don't follow the game, I'm unable to join the conversation, but Zander seems quite impressed with her knowledge.

One hour turns to two, and as the third hour approaches, a man dressed in scrubs pokes his head in. We all jump to our feet.

"I'm Dr. McNeill, and George did just fine. We had to put a rod and a few screws in, so I hope he's not planning to go through airport security anytime soon." We laugh at that, but all feel a measure of relief. "He'll be in recovery for a couple hours, and then he'll be moved to his own room for overnight observations. Tomorrow, he'll likely be able to go home."

"Thank you," Mom says, and for the first time since I've arrived, I notice how tired and drained she seems. The doctor leaves and we all sit again. "Why don't you two go home. No sense in all of us sitting here."

"I'm not going anywhere," I say.

"I'm staying too."

She points a finger at Zander. "You, young man, are not meeting George tonight. We'll save this surprise for the BBQ."

He gives mom a strange look, and I explain the heart attack comment from earlier. Zander laughs, and Mom excuses herself to go find the restrooms.

Zander cups my chin. "You okay?"

"I am now. You didn't have to come here, Zander."

"Yeah, I did. You went white, Sam. I was worried about you."

My heart pinches. "It's just...Dad, you know?"

"I do know," he says, and I rest my head on his shoulder.

"I'd be lost without him."

"A girl needs her dad," he says, and I put my arms around him and hold on tight.

"Thanks for coming to my rescue when Mom brought up grandkids."

"She's not very subtle, is she?"

I laugh at that. "Not a bit."

"You have a tendency to blurt things out, too."

"I am my mother's daughter," I say. I breathe in his scent and absorbs his strength as he continues to hold me. "The accident was kind of a wakeup call though."

"How so?"

"When I thought it was worse, that I could have actually lost dad, it made me think about my life...where I'm at and where I want to be. I'm not sure I'm ready for kids right now, but maybe I should visit the clinic, see what I might have to do down the road to give Dad the grandkids he wants." He stiffens slightly beside me, and I lift my head. "What?" I ask. "You don't think it's a good idea?"

"It's not that. I just want you to be sure. Have kids for *you*, not for any other reason."

"I do want kids...eventually," I say, and then drop the subject when Mom comes back into the room. A few more hours pass and a nurse comes by to let us know Dad has settled into his room.

"I'll be here waiting when you get back," he says softly into my ear.

"Thank you."

I put my arm around Mom and we follow the nurse to the room Dad is sharing with another patient. He's groggy when we reach him but alert enough to know who we are.

His arm is bandaged and hanging from some contraption. Things look dire, but I remind myself it could have been so much worse.

"Dad," I say and kiss his cheek. "How are you?" Stupid question, I know.

"Don't worry about me," he says. He glances heavenward. "He's taking care of me."

Mom settles on the other side of him. "You scared us half to death."

"How is the other driver?" he asks, and isn't that just like Dad, always worried and taking care of everyone else. At the end of the day, Zander is a lot like my father.

We talk for a few more minutes, but he's tired from the surgery and drugs, so we give him a kiss and make our way back to Zander. He jumps up when he sees us.

"How is he?"

"He's going to be just fine," I say.

"Glad to hear it. Mary, can I drive you home," Zander asks, and once again my heart pinches at his consideration. "I can pick you up tomorrow to come back and get your car."

"I cabbed it here. I was in no shape to drive. I can cab home."

"I won't hear of it," he says.

Mom opens her mouth to protest but I cut her off.

"Forget it, Mom. He's bossy and argumentative, and always wins out in the end."

"It's true," he says, and Mom laughs.

"In that case, I'll save my breath. Let's go." She walks out the door and heads to the elevators. Zander puts his arm around me, and I thank him as we follow behind.

We step into the warm night and Zander takes us to his car. I settle Mom in the front and I climb into the back.

"Where to?" he asks, and I give him directions. Half an hour later, we're at my childhood home, and Zander and I see that Mom gets inside safely. Once she's settled, I put the kettle on to boil for her nightly tea, give her a kiss and promise to call first thing in the morning.

Exhaustion from a long night, combined with stress, pulls at me as we climb back into the car.

"You're beat," he says.

"I am." I'm not about to deny it.

"You never even had dinner."

"You're right. I never thought about that." The last thing we had was ice cream. "Did you eat?"

"No, but Quinn said she'd feed Daisy, and since I didn't know how long I'd be, she's keeping her overnight." He reaches across the seat and squeezes my leg. "Why don't we go back to my place? You look like you could use a good long soak in the hot tub, and I can whip us up something to eat."

"You're tired, too. Let me order food in."

"Do you like Italian?"

"Carbs, only my favorite," I say, and he laughs.

"I'll order from Luigi's, it's my favorite. I won't get any garlic bread though. I'm not taking a risk of you not kissing me."

I chuckle softly. "It's going to take a whole lot more than garlic to keep me from kissing you."

...from falling for you.

16

ZANDER

Darkness has fallen over the city as I pull into my driveway and kill the ignition. I cast a glance Sam's way. "Doing okay?"

"I am. I think I'm just really tied from the adrenaline crash."

"I can imagine. Stay there, I'll come get you."

"I'm quite capable—"

"And I'm quite capable of coming to get you."

"So bossy," she says but sits still. I circle the car, help her from her seat and wrap my arm around her as I guide her inside. The lights are low, and I keep them that way. "Why don't you strip off, jump in the hot tub, and I'll put our food order in and join you."

"Done," she says.

"Not going to argue?"

"Nope." She peels her top off as she walks toward the back door, and I grab my cell and order all my favorites. I find two goblets, fill them with wine, and step outside.

"Mmm," she moans and runs her hands around the water. "This is glorious."

I set the wine down, strip off and join her. "Food will be about thirty minutes."

"I will be a prune by then." She glances my way. "I feel bad that you had to take Daisy to Quinn's though. I know you like to spend all your time with her."

"It's okay. Since she's been home with me all week, she hasn't seen Scotty, and misses him. I can't believe he didn't catch the chickenpox from her."

"I think sometimes it's just better to get them early and get them over with."

"True. Quinn and I had them at the same time."

"It must be hard being on the road, Zander. Being away from Daisy."

He takes a sip of wine and sets it aside. "It is. But I have a full-time nanny and Quinn. It's not the same as Daisy having a mother, but we make it work. I try to Skype with her as much as I can."

She shifts closer to me, and we lay our heads back to stare at the stars. "When are you playing a pickup game with the guys?" she asks.

"Funny you should ask. Jonah texted me earlier, to let me know it was tomorrow. I don't have to go. If you want me to take you to the hospital to see your father."

"No, I want you to go. I want to go, too. Does Quinn ever go? Maybe we can take the kids and go together."

I smile at that. "I'm sure Daisy would love that. Then maybe we could all come back for a barbeque. Quinn is away for the fourth, and she always has the family gathering, but she won't be here next weekend, so maybe we can all have an early celebration."

"That would be fun."

"I'll shoot Quinn a text when we finish here."

I take her hand in mine and she turns to me. I find her mouth for a slow, lingering kiss, one that feels far more emotional than physical. She relaxes into me, and we both go quiet for a moment, lost in our own thoughts.

My mind trips back to her wanting to visit a fertility clinic. I'm not sure why the idea of that bothers me so much. Maybe because Daisy will never know her mother, and I know how much she's missing out on. I'm not saying I want Shari back in our lives, not the way she currently is, but I don't want my child to ever have abandonment issues. Sam is young, and sweet, and everything a man could ask for.

"Why do you think you ruin all relationships?" I ask.

She stirs beside me, the question obviously catching her by surprise. "I'm not good with relationships, Zander."

"Tell me what happened."

A long pause, and then, "The first guy I dated... Well, I thought I loved him. I was young and stupid. I blurted it out one night, and that was the last I saw of him. I have a problem with my mouth, obviously."

I touch her lips, run my thumb over them. "Not as far as I can see," I say.

"The second guy I was serious with said I studied too hard, and I hadn't paid him enough attention. I never could get the whole work/life balance thing figured out, so in the end, I opted for work."

"You do realize this isn't on you, Sam. You were being honest and open, and those guys were chickenshits, simple as that. And as far as work/life balance, maybe the asshole should have been supporting you, and helping make things easier so you could pass your exams and step into the career you were chasing. Instead, he acted like a spoiled prick." I tamp down the anger. "*None* of this is on you, and there *is* someone out there for you. Someone who will give you the baby you want, and will listen to what you need."

She nods her head and looks off into the distance, like

she's really contemplating that. I hear the faint ding of the doorbell.

"Looks like our food is here."

"Have we been out here that long?"

"Time flies when you're having fun." I climb from the hot tub, tug on my jeans, and grab my wallet from the back pocket as I make my way to the foyer. Garlicy smells of bread and pasta fill the entranceway when I pull open the door.

The driver hands over the food. I paid with my card over the phone, but reach into my wallet to give him a generous tip.

"Hey, thanks, man," he says, then stands there for a moment. "Would you...uh...mind if I got a picture with you."

"Not at all."

The kid grabs his phone, and I smile as he takes a selfie of us. His grin is ear to ear as he shoves his phone back into his pocket. "The guys are going to lose their shit when I show them this."

He darts back to his car, and I shake my head as I close the door and turn to find Sam watching me from the kitchen, wrapped in nothing but a towel.

"That was nice of you."

I shrug. "It was nothing."

"You just made his day. Probably his year."

"Happy to do it." I walk to the kitchen and start pulling containers from the bag.

"It really is nothing to you, is it?" she says.

"What do you mean?"

"You're famous, Zander. People throw themselves at you, go crazy when they see you, and you just take it all in stride."

"I'm just a guy who made it to the NHL, Sam."

"With a lot of hard work and practice. Quinn told me how hard you worked. Wait, is that why they call you the Hard Hitter?"

"It's because I'm a power forward and have a powerful flick." I mimic the action of shooting the puck.

"You must score a lot."

I lift my head and grin at her. "I score enough."

She rolls her eyes and pulls out two plates, very familiar with where things are in my kitchen now. "Are we even talking about hockey anymore?"

I laugh at that. "Of course we are."

"I somehow doubt it."

I divvy up the pasta, and bread. "Want to eat in the living room, watch a movie?"

"I would love that." We make our way to the living room, and I flick on the television. Some chick flick that she seems excited about comes on, and I place my plate on my lap and dig in.

"This is so good," she says, her eyes wide, full of delight.

"Better than those microwave dinners you eat?"

"Yes, but they have way less calories."

"Sam, you're perfect just the way you are." She gives me a small kiss on the cheek, and warmth settles in my chest, right around the vicinity of my heart. "What was that for?"

"No reason," she says.

We both turn back to the TV and finish our meals. I shift on the sofa and pull her to me. We stay snuggled until the movie ends, and I carry her to my room. It's still early enough for me to shoot a text off to Quinn to ask about Daisy, and see if she's up for watching the game tomorrow. I do that as Sam makes her way to the bathroom to get ready for bed. My gaze is latched onto her body as she walks away, and I can't deny that it feels so right to have her here in my bed...my home.

Quinn texted back that they're in, and that Daisy and Scotty are fast asleep, and that she noticed Daisy was doing so much better with her 's' words. I smile at that.

Sam comes from the bathroom, dressed only in her bra and underwear. I gave her a toothbrush, but that's the extent of her belongings here. "You're going to have to start keeping clothes here," I say to her.

She frowns.

"What?"

"Oh, nothing. Just thinking about my father," she answers, and while I don't doubt that, I sense there is more going on with her. Could she be changing her mind on relationships?

If so, is she thinking we could make one work?

Is that even what I want?

Changing the subject, I say, "My buddies and their wives can make the BBQ, and Quinn is up for both the game and BBQ, and she said she noticed Daisy is much better with her words."

That brings a smile to her face. "That makes me so happy."

She settles into the bed, and I head toward the bathroom to take my turn. "Why speech therapy? What made you choose that field of study?"

I put toothpaste on my brush and run it under the water. I move back to the doorway to hear her answer, but her nose is crinkled and she's plucking at an imaginary piece of lint on the sheet.

"Sam?"

"I... When I was younger, I had a stutter," she says.

"Really. I wouldn't have known." I take a moment to think about that. When we first met, sometimes she would pause during speech, like she was trying to formulate her words. The more time we spent together, the less she did it.

She flattens the sheet over her thighs, and runs her palms along them to smooth them out. "It was bad, and I was embarrassed by it."

I stop brushing. "I'm sorry."

"I was teased, relentlessly, and I guess I just wanted to help other children avoid the pain that comes with being different."

My heart wobbles slightly. This woman is seriously too good to be true. "I had no idea." I walk back to the sink and finish brushing. She's fixing her pillow when I get into bed. "Kids can be so cruel."

"Adults, too."

I take in the pained look in her eyes, and my body stiffens. "What happened?"

"My stutter can come back when I'm emotionally distressed. When my ex broke off the engagement, called me horrible names, it came back with a vengeance, and it honestly took days for me to pull myself together."

My fingers curl into fists. "If I ever meet him—"

"It's okay, I'm over it. I try not to let my emotions get the best of me like that anymore."

"It's okay if you stutter, Sam."

"Justin wanted the perfect minister's daughter. He never heard me stutter until the night I asked for rough sex, and he degraded me for it. I think the stutter sealed the deal for him walking, but like I said, in the end, I'm better off for it. I can only be me, and if he didn't like me for me, then so be it."

"It was definitely his loss."

"I agree," she says with a lift of her chin.

"Atta girl," I say, and give her chin a nudge with my fist. In that moment, something passes between us, some deeper understanding of one another, empathy...a stronger friendship.

I tug her down beneath me, and press a soft kiss to her mouth. She opens for me instantly, and we taste the depths of each other. I remove her clothes, slowly this time, memorizing every inch of her curvy body. I kiss her from head to toe and back up again, and before I know it, her mouth is on *my* body, kissing and licking, savoring every inch.

"I need to be inside you," I say, and flip her over onto her back, desperate to see her face, her eyes when she comes for me. I push into her in one hard thrust, but then with unhurried movements, I slide in and out, a tender, intimate joining.

We move together, our two bodies becoming one, and even though our lovemaking is slower this time, it's every bit as profound—maybe even more so—than the last times.

Wait!

Lovemaking?

17

SAM

Daisy sits on my lap and wiggles as she watches her daddy effortlessly go from one end of the ice to the other, the puck on the end of his stick.

"Daddy, Daddy," she calls out, but he can't hear her as he races the long length of the rink, his eyes latched on the net. A couple of local teenage boys and girls who were at the rink have joined them, and I can just imagine how excited they must be to play with these NHL superstars.

"I can't believe you've never watched hockey before," Quinn says.

"Me neither, it's kind of fun."

Quinn laughs at me and opens a juice pack for both the kids. She hands one to Daisy, and Daisy climbs from my lap to settle into the seat next to me like a big girl.

"You're not cold, are you?" I ask her. We packed hats and mittens and are in our heavy sweaters, but I can't remember the last time I'd been in a rink, and really had no idea what to expect.

"Dad is seriously going to freak out when he meets

Zander. It's going to be embarrassing, I can tell you that much."

"No worries. Zander takes everything in stride. He won't let the situation become embarrassing. He's good at that."

"He's good at a lot of things," I say, very impressed watching him protect the puck. "How does he even do that?" I lean forward, my eyes on the Hard Hitter as he shoots and scores. His teammates clap him on the back, and Jonah skates around him, shoving him up against the boards. Today they're on opposite teams, and it's quite funny to watch them compete.

"He has a way with people." I nod, and Quinn continues, "Your Dad, he's doing okay? I was so sorry to hear about his accident."

I nod. "Mom went in early this morning, and he's home now resting." I chuckle. "He'll milk this injury for all it's worth and have Mom running her feet off. I'll be by to help out as well."

Her smile is soft, warm when she says, "It's nice that you guys are all so close."

"It really is," I say.

"Zander has always wanted that for me and Daisy. But I think he forgets that it's something he wants, too."

"He does?"

"Yeah, he'd love to have a big happy family, but sadly, he's resigned himself to the fact that it's never going to happen."

My heart squeezes at that. I want so much for Zander. He's an amazing guy, so caring, giving, always putting the needs of others first. He deserves the world and then some.

The guys carry on in the rink, and Daisy grows antsy beside me.

Quinn reaches for her diaper bag. "We should probably get them out of here. Scotty needs a diaper change."

"Why don't we head back to my place." As soon as the

words leave my mouth, I catch myself. I've been spending a lot of time at Zander's, and feel very comfortable there, but it's definitely *not* my place, even though he'd given me a key. "I mean *Zander's* place. I have a lot of prep for the barbeque."

"Sounds great. I'll help."

I scoop up Daisy and Zander glances over at me. He knew we might leave early, since we had the kids. "Wave bye to Daddy," I say to Daisy, and as we both wiggle our fingers, Zander goes still, a change coming over him.

He removes his helmet, and intense eyes lock with mine.

Beside me, Quinn is packing up the toys and juice boxes, and doesn't notice...but there is something going on with Zander. I can feel it deep in my soul.

Jonah skates up to him, and it seems to pull Zander from whatever trance he was in.

We make our way to the entrance, and both Zander and Jonah come off the ice. Zander drops a kiss onto Daisy's cheek.

"You guys heading out?" he asks.

"Quinn and I are going to make the salads and get the steaks marinated. Take your time, have fun, we have everything covered."

"You sure?"

"Positive. I like doing this for you, Zander. You do so much for me, and everyone else."

"Okay, we won't be too long." Our eyes hold, linger, but he doesn't kiss me, not in front of his daughter and the other guys.

I'm about to turn when I get a sharp pain in my stomach. I lean forward, and a noise crawls out of my throat.

Zander quickly takes Daisy from me. "Are you okay?" he asks, and when I straighten, the concern on his face fills my heart with all the things I'm not supposed to feel for this man.

"Cramp," I say. "A girl thing."

He nods and puts Daisy down. "I want you to walk, Daisy."

"Okay, Daddy," she says, and when she reaches up and takes my hand, the muscles along Zander's jaw tighten. I hold her tiny little hand, and my heart beats a bit harder. Walking away from Zander...from Daisy...is going to be a lot harder than I ever expected.

"You sure you're okay? Daisy might be too heavy for you. You might have strained something."

"No, I'm pretty sure it's a girl thing," I say.

I turn to see Jonah handing Scotty back to Quinn and after the guys see us off, we pile into Quinn's car, which always has a spare seat for Daisy. The kids play in the back as Quinn drives us to Zander's place, and from the way she's casting me glances, I get that she has something on her mind.

"What?" I finally ask.

She laughs. "You like him."

"Like who?" I ask, playing dumb as we pass through the elite neighborhood.

"My brother."

"Of course I like him. He's a nice guy."

"You *like him*, like him."

I go quiet and think about that. Yes, I do *like him* like him. I should have known better than to get involved with a guy like Zander. But at first I didn't know how sweet and caring he was under that perfect muscular package and handsome face.

I think back to what he said about all my ex-boyfriends. He said none of it was on me, that it wasn't me who ruined things. Was he right? I don't know, but I'm scared to try. If I really gave Zander my heart and in the end, I messed things up, I'm not so sure I could ever be put back together again.

But if I don't try, don't ever see where we could go, I could spend the rest of my life asking what if.

Then another though hits.

What does Zander want?

He's as afraid of love as I am, has had so many women turn their back on him, on Daisy. Does he think I'm the type who would do that?

Quinn pulls into Zander's driveway and turns to me. "Why so quiet?"

I plaster on a smile and reach for the door handle. "Just thinking," I say, and I'm glad when she doesn't push it. We gather the kids, and for a brief second I imagine what life would be like if Daisy was mine, if I did live here with Zander, and got to hang out with Quinn all the time. It all feels so real and wonderful...and the scariest thing about that visual is just how much I want it.

We take the kids inside and she takes Scotty upstairs to change him, while I settle Daisy at the kitchen table with a coloring book. She sits quietly and mumbles about *Paw Patrol*, and Scotty smelling bad, and talks about a few of her other friends at the daycare. My heart trembles for the child. It must be so incredibly hard on her when her daddy is away at hockey.

Quinn comes back, and Daisy drops to the floor with Scotty to play with some toys. "I think Scotty needs a sibling," Quinn says, and looks up at me with a grin on her face.

"Wait...what are you telling me?"

She chuckles and steps closer. "Don't say anything, it's early yet," she says, putting her hand on her stomach. "We're not telling anyone until the third trimester but...I'm pregnant. We just found out, and if I didn't soon tell someone I was going to burst!"

I pull my friend into my arms and give her a big hug. Tears prick my eyes. "I'm so happy for you, Quinn."

"I like the idea of having them close in age. It won't be easy, but I want them to be best friends, like Zander and I are. And I'm sure Daisy will love to have another cousin, especially another girl to play with." Quinn smiles as Daisy hands Scotty a toy.

"She will," I say. "I was an only child and would have loved to have a brother or a sister."

"Well, you're here with Zander, so you can consider *me* your sister," she says, and gives me another hug that nearly has me crying like a baby.

I sniff to hide it, and when she pulls away, I ask, "Are you going to tell, Zander?"

"Jonah is. He probably already has."

Needing a reprieve from all the emotions welling up inside me, I point to the fridge. "Okay, we'd better get the salads ready before the guys get back."

"Look at you, putting a pregnant lady to work." She laughs and opens the fridge. "Have you ever thought about having kids?" she asks. We're friends, but we've never really discussed this topic before.

"I have," I say, but don't elaborate. She doesn't need to know that I've been thinking about a clinic. I'm sure most people would balk at the idea. We make small talk and fix the salads and marinate the steak. By the time we're done, the kids are fussing.

"Hey Scotty, how about a fast swim and then a nap," Quinn says as she picks him up.

"I don't want a nap," Daisy says.

"How about a swim then," I say, and wink at Quinn. Daisy is rubbing her tired little eyes, and playtime in the pool will certainly wear her out more.

"Wait, I don't have a suit," I say.

"I have extras. We're about the same size."

"Uh, not really."

"You have more curves than me, which, by the way, I'm quite jealous of."

"Oh, please."

"I'm serious." She puts her hands on my hips. "I would kill for these. Come on, let's get the kids changed, and I'll hook you up with a suit. I keep extras here, didn't Zander tell you?"

"No, he didn't."

"Of course he didn't. Lured you into skinny dipping, did he?" She laughs out loud at that, and color moves into my cheeks.

"He's going to pay for that," I say, as I follow her up the steps.

She goes into one of the many spare rooms, and I follow her. "I used to stay here a lot when Daisy first came to live with Zander. I have a bunch of my clothes in here if you ever need anything." She sits Scotty on the bed and I sit Daisy beside him. Quinn pulls out a few bathing suits and holds them out for my inspection.

"I think that one will do," I say, and point to the one with the most fabric. I scoop it up and take Daisy to her room to get changed. I help her into her suit, climb into mine, which is a bit snug, and we meet Quinn and Scotty at the pool. The water is glorious on this hot afternoon, and before we know it, we've been in for close to an hour. Scotty's eyes are rolling back in his head.

"I think this one needs a nap," she says.

"Daisy, how about we get changed too. I wouldn't mind lying down on your bed." I stretch my arms out. "I'm so tired!"

"Okay," she says, and when we climb from the pool, the sound of voices reaches our ears. Dammit, I was hoping to be back in my clothes before all the guys arrived.

Zander comes through the door first, and his eyes dart to mine, then slowly move down the length of me. A bit self-conscious in the skimpy suit, I fold my arms across my chest. Jonah and the three other guys they were playing hockey with follow Zander outside.

Zander walks over to me, effectively blocking me from the other men. "Hey," he says. "Nice suit."

"Quinn lent it to me. Apparently, she keeps a few of them here."

He grins. "I forgot about that."

"I'm sure you did."

He bends and picks up a tired Daisy. "Did you have a fun day?"

She nods and rubs her eyes.

"She was just going to take me upstairs for a nap," I say.

Zander nods in understanding. "How about I help you get Sam to bed," he says to his daughter, and she nods again.

We all go upstairs, and Zander dresses Daisy as I climb back into my clothes. I crawl into bed, and Daisy lays down beside me. Her fingers go to my hair again, and Zander watches us for a moment, once again his jaw tight.

"Give me a minute," I whisper to him. He nods and steps into the hall. I relax in the small bed, and soon enough, Daisy's breathing changes, becomes slower, softer. I move gently and check on her. I smile and brush her hair from her face, and carefully climb from the tiny bed. In the hall, I find Zander waiting for me.

Catching me off guard, he pulls me to him and gives me a long, deep kiss that messes with my ability to stand. He breaks the kiss and says, "That's for coming to the game and bringing Daisy. Did you enjoy it?"

"I loved it."

"Sorry about you having to do all the prep work for dinner. It was my idea. I should have been the one in the kitchen."

"I didn't mind at all. I'm happy you got to hang out with

the guys. Besides, I had the kids and Quinn to keep me company."

He puts his arm around me and leads me down the stairs. "Speaking of Quinn," he says quietly. "Did she share her news?"

I nod. "I'm so happy for them."

"Me too," he says, and from his wide smile, it's easy to see how proud he is of his sister.

We step outside, and his friend Jamie presses a beer into Zander's hand, and Quinn hands me a glass of wine.

"Now that everyone is here," Jamie, says.

"What's going on?" I quietly ask Quinn.

"Apparently Jamie has an announcement to make."

Jamie holds his beer up. "I wanted to let you know that I'm getting married!"

A chorus of "no fucking way" sounds from the guys, and I look around, wondering why that's so hard to believe.

"It's true. I'm getting married. Sara wanted to be here with me when I told you guys, but she's experiencing a bit of morning sickness and was worried about the flight. But I wanted to come and tell you all in person."

Another round of "no fucking way" sounds from the guys.

"Marriage and a baby," Jonah says, adding a low, slow whistle. "Never thought I'd see the day. I'll drink to that," he says, and everyone lifts their glasses.

My eyes go to Zander as we all clink. He stares back, his eyes a stormy blue on this calm Saturday afternoon.

"Congratulations," Zander says, breaking my gaze and turning to his friend. "I can't believe Sara finally wrestled you into submission. It wasn't that long ago you said you were going to be a bachelor for life."

"When the right girl comes around, you know it," Jamie says. "And don't worry, Zander. One of these days, you'll wake up married with a houseful of kids.

18

ZANDER

"Why are you so nervous?" I ask as I shoot a glance Sam's way, taking in the way she's nibbling her bottom lip. I reach across the seat and give her elbow a reassuring squeeze.

From the passenger seat beside me, she slowly turns her head my way, and I scrub my hand over my freshly shaved face, wanting to present my best self to her family.

"You're Zander Reed, and my dad is going to go ballistic. So are my uncles and cousins."

I shrug, but I'm not convinced that's what on her mind. For the last week, ever since we'd hosted a BBQ for my friends, she's been quieter than unusual.

"Don't worry about it, Sam. I'm just a guy going to your Fourth of July barbeque. I'm no different than any of the other guys."

"You're an NHL superstar. That makes you different."

"Not to me." She adjusts the tea towel under the casserole dish full of ribs she cooked at my place, and I redirect the conversation. "Those smell good," I say. "I can't wait to dig in."

"Only my famous BBQ ribs," she says with a lift of her chin. "And don't pretend that you haven't already tasted one. I saw you sneaking one earlier, and you still have sauce on your face."

I grab the rearview mirror to check. "No, I don't," I say.

She's laughing when I glance back at her. "No, you don't, and I didn't see you sneak one, but now I know for sure you did."

"You're going to pay for that," I tease.

"Can't wait," she says. "I don't cook much but these are Dad's favorites. He's going to make quite the mess eating them with one hand."

"What is the doc saying?"

"He'll be in a cast for a few more weeks, but things are progressing nicely. He'll be as good as new. Thank God. He gave us a good scare there."

"Daddy, I'm hungry," Daisy says from the backseat, and kicks her legs out.

"Almost there," I say, knowing the way from when I drove Sam's mom home from the hospital last weekend. Sam has dropped by her parents' place every night this week, and I love how much she cares for them. After her visits, she always ended up at my place, with a good long commute back to her place for work in the morning.

I hate that she has to drive, but it's easier for us to have Daisy in her own home, and Sam swears she doesn't mind. During the day, while Daisy is at daycare with Quinn, I've been hanging out at Sam's doing some much-needed repairs to her place. She'd even given me my own key, enabling me to come and go as I please, and she kept her end of the bargain up. Pie every day.

"I want to play with Scotty," Daisy says.

"She needs a sibling," Sam blurts out—and then instantly stiffens.

"Sam," I begin, even though I'm not sure what it is I want to say. Perhaps I want to tell her I agree, that Daisy does need a sibling, but that she also needs a mother...and ask if maybe she's willing to take on that roll...maybe both. But she's a girl not interested in relationships, and I've been telling her I have serious trust issues.

Do I trust Sam?

"I mean...oh, never mind. I guess I was just thinking about Quinn being pregnant. I think it's great they want to give Scotty a sibling. I wasn't suggesting..." She lets her words fall off, and glances over her shoulder. "Don't worry, Daisy. There are going to be lots of kids for you to play with."

"Yay!" she says and claps her hands.

"Have you given any more thoughts about having a kid?" I ask quietly, and clench my jaw until my muscles are tight. When it comes right down to it, I hate the thought of her going to a clinic. A girl like Sam needs a nice guy, one who will be there for her and her baby.

"A little bit, especially after Quinn telling me she's pregnant. I think it got my maternal clock ticking."

I give a tight nod and stare straight ahead. Daisy turns on her iPad and begins to sing along to that alligator song that makes me want to hang myself. I'll have an earworm all day now. Since we're unable to talk over the noise, we drive in silence, and when I reach her childhood home and find the driveway full, I pull up to the curb and park. I glance at the house, hear laugher coming from the backyard, and longing pulls at me.

Her house is small, and quaint, and full of love. I want this for Daisy so much.

I want this for me.

"You sure you still want to do this?" she asks, and crinkles that cute little nose of her.

"I'm game, but are you sure you still *want* me to do this?"

She nods. "I think so."

I pitch my voice low. "Remember the rules, though."

Her mouth drops open. "You didn't tell me there were rules."

I laugh at her horrified expression. "There are going to be question, lots of questions. If you want your family to get off your back, to show Caleb you're taken, we have to pretend we're a couple. A real couple."

What the fuck am I doing?

Oh, I don't know, maybe trying it on for size, just to see how it fits.

She flips her hands over. "Well, yeah, I knew we were going to pretend we were together, but—"

"There will have to be touching, Sam. Public displays of affections. That's what couple do."

"You...want to touch me, in front of everyone?"

"I always want to touch you. In front of your family or not."

Pink crawls up her neck, and it's all I can do not to lean over and kiss her, but I have my daughter in the car and need to be careful.

"We better get in there before they send a search party."

We all exit the car, and I scoop Daisy into my arms. We go up the small walkway, but Sam comes to an abrupt halt and leans forward slightly, balancing the casserole in her hands as air leaving her lungs in a whoosh.

"What's wrong?" I ask when she straightens, my stomach tightening at how pale she's gone.

"Cramps," she says again.

Unease moves through me. Back in the day, Quinn got irritable and complained of cramps, but I don't ever remember her nearly dropping to her knees. "Is that normal, Sam?"

"Yes," she says. "It's why I'm on the pill."

"It doesn't seem to be helping."

"You're right. I think I should probably make an appointment." She blinks and shakes her head. "It passed."

"You sure you don't want to go back home and lie down?"

"Mom would kill me if we didn't come."

"If at any time you don't feel well, I'll take you home, Okay? You just say the word."

She nods, takes the three steps to the front door, and I pull open the screen door and follow her into her parents' home. I smile as I take it in again. I'd only gotten a fast glimpse when I'd given Mary a ride home. The place is warm, cozy, with lots of pictures of Sam when she was young. This is the kind of house every kid deserves to grow up in.

"Don't look at those," she says as we go down the hall toward the kitchen, where I hear a bunch of women talking and laughing. The sound fills my heart with warmth.

"Look, Daisy. That's Sam when she was your age."

Daisy giggles, and Sam shoots me a warning glare. I laugh and follow along, and all heads turn our way when we enter the small kitchen.

"We're here," Sam says.

"About time," her mother says lovingly, then her eyes turn to Daisy and me. "Zander, so nice to see you again." She walks up to me and puts her hands on either side of Daisy's face. "And who is this precious girl?"

"This is Daisy. Daisy, say hello to Mrs. Peters. Mrs. Peters is Sam's mom."

"Oh, phooey, you call me Mary," she says, and Daisy touches her cheeks, and squeezes them together in guppy manner. Mary laughs and makes guppy faces, and Daisy giggles.

"You look like Andi!"

"Andi is her goldfish," I explain.

"I love goldfish," Mary says. Then, taking me by surprise, Daisy holds her arms out for Mary to take her.

The second she does, an instant bond is created between the two, one so strong I feel it all the way to my core. My throat dries as Mary fusses with my girl and carries her to the table, where many of the others are seated and prepping the food. As Mary offers Daisy a small cookie, tells her about the children outside who can't wait to meet her, I try to breathe, but can't seem to pull any air into my lungs.

"Zander, you okay?" Sam asks, her eyes moving over mine.

"Fine," I say, pulling myself together. "Hey everyone, I'm Zander." I glance at Daisy, who is lost in conversation with Mary, telling her some story about Scotty—and that's when it really occurs to me that she no longer has a lisp.

She'll no longer need visits with Sam—which means our time together is up.

"I'm Sam's boyfriend," I blurt out.

A brief moment of silence ensues—save for Daisy telling Mary a dramatic story about something Scotty did at daycare —and then a million questions are thrown at us, like how we met, how long we've been together, what our future plans are, and if we plan to have children. These women hold nothing back, and that actually amuses me. Sam has good people in her life, people who truly care for her and her well-being, and that makes me happy.

Sam holds her hands up to cut everyone off. "He's not here for an interrogation. No more questions. Let the poor man breathe."

"The guys are outside," Mary says, gesturing toward the patio doors. "Make sure your father is sitting down before you introduce Zander, we don't need another emergency trip to the hospital." Mary turns her attention back to Daisy. "Now Daisy, would you be a dear and help us bring the food outside?" Daisy nods, her curls bouncing. "Do you like hot dogs?" Mary asks.

"With ketchup," Daisy says.

"Perfect," Mary says as she beams at my child.

"She's fine here with mom," Sam says. "Want to go meet the guys?"

I reach for her hand, a public display of affection—something we don't ever do, except for the time I gave her a comforting hug at the hospital—and she seems surprised at first, but then she softens beneath my touch, likely remembering the rules. But I can't say for sure I'm holding her hand because we need to touch for show. No, I'm pretty sure seeing Daisy with Sam's mother, a woman who would dearly love grandkids and would be so amazing with them, is gutting me from the inside out.

Daisy is missing out on so much.

Sam leads me through the back patio door, and the men are joking and laughing. Some are playing horseshoes, or tossing bean bags with the younger kids, and others are standing around the barbecue, talking sports. Sam's father—and I only assume he's her father because he's in a cast—is alternating between flipping food on the grill and drinking a beer with his free hand.

"Dad," Sam says, but her voice is drowned out by someone laughing. "Dad," she says again, a little louder this time.

Her father turns, and his eyes fill with love when they see her. I know the feeling; it's one I get every time I see Daisy. It brings warmth to my soul as I watch the exchange. His gaze slowly leaves Sam's and settles on me. He stares at me for a moment, like he's trying to place me, then a light bulb goes off, and he stumbles.

Sam hurries to him and wraps her arms around his waist.

"Dad, this is Zander. Zander, this is my dad George."

He puts his hand to his chest—and now I'm a bit worried Mary wasn't kidding about the heart attack. "Your mother said you were bringing someone but I had no idea it was going to be Zander Reed. *The* Zander Reed!"

"It's just Zander Reed, or rather, Zander," I say, and reach for the man's hand. He gives me a good firm shake, still staring at me like he can't believe I'm real.

"Dad, relax," Sam says, and pinches him. "It's just Zander."

George shakes his head to pull himself together as all eyes focus on me. "Where are my manners?" he says. "Come meet the family." He introduces me to Uncle Don, Charlie, Freddie, Doug and Bill, and I pray to God there isn't going to be a test. There are too many faces to remember. Then the cousins and children are all introduced, and finally, I meet Caleb.

He has a twisted scowl on his face when he takes my hand, but I keep things polite.

"Nice to meet you, Caleb."

"I didn't know Sam was dating."

I reach for Sam, pull her to me, and her hand goes to my stomach, her touch racing right through me and settling around my heart.

"I see he's still alive," Mary says as she comes from the kitchen, breaking the awkward silence. Beside her, Daisy is carrying a small dish that she sets on the table. "This is Daisy, everyone. Zander's daughter. She's such a great helper in the kitchen." Daisy beams up at Mary, and Mary looks like she's in heaven. The woman really does need grandkids. I guess now I can see why Sam is thinking of a fertility clinic—especially after her father's scare. Her child would be the luckiest in the world to be surrounded by people like these.

A couple of young girls walk over to Daisy and they take

her hands, bringing her to the garden to play. I watch for a moment, my heart so full, I'm sure I'm going to crack a rib.

Just then, George throws his arm around me like we're old pals.

"Now, let's talk about last season, son," he says, and my throat squeezes.

Son?

I haven't been called son, or felt a part of anything special like this in...forever.

"Dad," Sam warns.

"It's fine, Sam," I say, and when someone puts a bottle of craft beer in my hand, I take a long pull. I check the label and don't recognize it. "Double hopped IPA. Damn, that's good." That's when I remember George is a minister. "Oh, sorry. I didn't mean to swear," I say, and Sam is biting back a smile.

George grins. "No worries, son." He clinks his bottle with mine. "We both like Sam and we both like the same beer. We're going to get along just fine. Now, let's talk about that move you made when playing the Warriors."

I cast a look Sam's way, catch her nibbling on her lips.

What is really going on with her? She's been distracted since last week. Was she worried about me meeting her family, or does she have something else on her mind?

I give her a nod to let her know I'm good, and she saunters off with the other women to set the table.

All the men huddle around me, and for the next half hour, as the food is cooking on the grill, we talk sports. It's fun, really, and I love that they're die-hard fans.

"Did you know Sam has never watched a game with me?" George asks, and shakes his head like he can't understand such a thing.

"She came to the rink last week. Rider, Kane, Jamie and Jonah and I played a game of pickup with a few of the local kids."

"That's it. I'm disowning you, Sam," he calls out, and Sam rolls her eyes. "Let me know next time. I want to come."

"You were kind of down and out in the hospital."

"You think that would keep me from a game?"

"No, I suppose not," I say, and hand him a plate when he gestures for it. I watch him struggle to get the meat from the grill, but I know a man with pride when I see it, so I don't offer to help.

The food is all laid out buffet style, and the kids come racing over. I kneel down next to Daisy. "What would you like to eat?"

"Oh, I don't mind helping her," Mary says. "Now come on, Daisy, let me get you that hot dog with ketchup."

Daisy slides her hand into Mary's and trots off with her. I stand there, loving the way Mary is fussing over her. Sam steps up beside me, and when I turn to her, and her dark eyes lock on mine, my entire world shifts.

I want this. I want all of this.

With Sam.

But would she want to be a part of our lives, or would she eventually regret the responsibility of a ready-made family and leave?

19

SAM

Zander has been in and out of my place all week, doing the repairs to my home while I work with my clients. Over a month has passed, and I'm still working with Daisy, even though she has now mastered her 's' words. But I'm not in a hurry to close her file. I like being with her, and Zander, have grown accustomed to having them in my life, and I'm not quite sure how I can let them go.

There has been no talk of extending our relationship past our agreed-upon terms, even though we've gone a little beyond our cutoff date. But as long as I'm treating Daisy, our affair continues.

Is it possible that Zander is in no hurry to move on either? Perhaps he'll want to continue to be with me until he has to leave for hockey, and then pick up again where we left off when he returns.

Do I dare wish for such a thing?

As I walk though my house, my work done for the day, a noise sounds at my door, and I saunter to it and pick up the mail that has been dropped through the slot. My stomach cramps slightly as I walk back to my kitchen, and I make a mental note to call my doctor, to get a checkup, and possible a pap test. I should have done it weeks ago, but I've been run off my feet during the day with my growing business, and spending my nights with Zander at his house.

Ever since the day of the BBQ in his backyard, seeing all his friends who were getting married or having babies, it's really made me reflect on my own life, and what I want out of it.

One thing is for certain—I don't have it in me to walk away from Zander and Daisy.

My heart lodges in my throat as I think about that. We're going to have to have a conversation, a deep and meaningful one, but I'm so afraid that Zander won't want more.

But what if he does?

I can't walk away without finding out.

As I flip through my mail, I think about my past relationships, and how they ended. Maybe I really didn't screw anything up at all. With Zander and I, things are going great, and I've not done anything to mess up this amazing relationship. Maybe I'm really not such a screwup after all.

One letter catches my eyes, and I tear into it and start reading out loud.

"We have reviewed your application carefully, and contacted your references. We would love for you to come interview for the applied position at our Houston campus. Please contact us at the number below to set up your interview." I smile as I read it. "Huh," I say, having never really expected to hear back from the university clinic.

I applied for the job a few months back, when I wanted to change jobs, but then I had a change of heart and went forth with the scary challenge of hanging my own sign. Things were tough at first, and they still are, but my name is getting out there and my slots are filling up quite nicely.

I toss the paper aside...and a wave of nausea hits me.

Slightly lightheaded, I drop into a wooden chair and take deep gulping breaths. I sit out the wave, and my eyes stray to my calendar, to note the date.

I sit up a little straighter as I do the mental math.

"Oh. My. God." I gulp, and do another quick calculation. "No. No. No," I say out loud.

I must be mistaken. I *have* to be mistaken.

Reaching for my purse, I dart outside, jump into my car and head to the nearest drugstore. My heart is racing so fast, it's pounding in my ears and blurring my vision. I'm breathless by the time I exit my car and hurry to the pharmacy. I search the shelves until I find what I'm looking for. I pay for it quickly, get back in my car, and speed home in record time.

My legs are shaky as I enter my house, and I'm grateful Zander isn't here to see what I'm about to do. I try to quiet my racing thoughts, but my efforts prove futile.

What if the results are positive?

My vision fades, and I sink against the wall. After everything Zander said to me, everything I said to him, would he think I'm trying to trap him, or I used his sperm to have my own baby without his permission? Dear God, I can't be pregnant. I just can't be! That would ruin everything that's been growing between Zander and me. Right?

Making my way to the bathroom, I tear into the package and read the instructions. Simple enough. I just pee on the stick and wait two minutes. I take down my pants and follow the instructions. Once done, I place the stick on the edge of the counter, pull up my pants and wash my hands. I pace the small bathroom, two steps one way, two steps back, and keep my eye on my phone.

My God, this is the slowest two minutes in my life.

My stomach cramps again, and as I brace my hands on the wall, the front door opens.

Oh, God no!

"Hey Sam, I grabbed the caulking to fix the tub." When I don't answer, heavy footsteps sound in the hall. "Sam?"

"I'm in here," I call out, hoping my voice doesn't sound as hysterical as I feel. "I'll be out in a minute."

I see the shadow of his feet underneath the door. "You okay?" he asks, his voice low, close to the door.

"Sure," I lie. The truth is, I want to be pregnant with Zander's baby as much as I don't want to be. I love him, love his daughter, and if I'm going to bring life into this world, I don't want to use a donor in a sterile clinic. I want the child to come from love.

Zander continues down the hall, and the back door opens. He must have gone out in to the yard. My phone passes the two-minute mark, and I still can't quite bring myself to look.

Do it already, Sam.

I suck in a fast breath, close my eyes and turn.

When I open them again, the bottom falls out of my world.

"What the fuck, Sam?" Zander suddenly says from outside the locked bathroom door. He rattles the knob, hard. "When the fuck were you going to tell me?"

My heart is pounding, tears beating against the back of my eyes. How the hell does he know? I'm in here behind a locked door!

"Say something," he demands.

"I was going to tell you," I say, my voice as shaky as my body.

"When?"

"I just found out."

"You just found out?" his anger reaches out to me, curls around my heart and squeezes until it I can't seem to breathe. "You must have applied months ago!"

Applied months ago?

"All this time, you knew you might be leaving for Houston and didn't think it was important to tell me?"

Houston.

Relief washes through me.

Eager to set him straight, that I applied ages ago and have no intention of going, I pull open the door. "I'm not—" I begin.

But his angry gaze drops from my face—to the stick I'm holding in my hand.

Oh, shit.

As things go from bad to worse, his throat works as he swallows, and the muscles along his jaw are so taut I swear they're going to snap.

"Zander—" I begin.

"What the *fuck*, Sam." The confusion, the hurt in his eyes, cuts like a dagger to my gut. He grips the doorjamb, and holds it tight as he take a few deep breaths.

I give him a moment to pull himself together—heck, I need a moment too—and then I hold the stick out. "I'm...pregnant."

"Yeah, I can see that." His head lifts, and the volatile storm washing black into blue hits like a punch to the jaw. I falter backward, reach behind me and grab the sink. "Is it mine?" he asks, this time his tone is cold, hard...angry. His words, and the harsh delivery, slice through me, leave me scraped raw and bleeding.

"Yes," I answer softly. "It's yours. I haven't been with anyone else. You know that, Zander."

He scoffs, like he doesn't believe me, and there is a part of me that can understand why. He'd been tricked and trapped before, but I'm not like those other women, would never do that to him. After everything, does he not realize that about me?

He shakes his head, and his nostrils flare. "You sure about that?"

No longer able to hold back the tears, they fall freely down my face, and when my legs give, I sink to the floor. "I didn't mean to get pregnant. I swear."

"Were you really on the pill?"

I press my hands to my face, hardly able to believe the things he's saying to me. This man knows me, the same way I know him. Does he really think I'm the kind of girl who would do this, whether to trap him *or* to give myself the baby I want? Does he think I'd use him like that? Does he think so little of me?

Apparently, he must.

"Were you?"

"Yes, I was...still am," I shoot back, anger moving though me. "It's not one hundred percent, you know. Sometime women can still get pregnant."

"What did your neighbor Katrina mean when she said she knew you *well enough*? Was she trying to warn me about what kind of woman you really are?"

I understand where his anger is coming from. I truly do, but he has to start believing in other people, and stop letting the past ruin his future. "I can't believe you're asking me that. Katrina is a mean girl, Zander. She clearly wanted you, and was just looking to fill you with doubt about me. It obviously worked."

"I don't know what to believe anymore. Things...the past. I've been fucked over before." He tosses the paper in his hand to the floor sucks in a fast breath and asks, "Were you just going to move, take the baby with you? I won't let you do that, Sam. If the baby is mine, I'll fight for my rights."

"No, it's not like that, Zander!" I say, things completely fucked up between us now.

"Then what is it like?"

"I...I..." I try to force the words out, but I can't talk. "I... y-you...w-we..."

I pound the floor as my emotions get the best of me and my stutter comes back full force. I try again, fight for my words, but it's no use.

"Right, okay then. You can't even tell me what it's like, can't even come up with a good lie. How about when you figure it out, you let me know," he says.

Turning, his boots stomp hard on the floor as he walks down the hall, and he slams the door behind him with so much force, it vibrates right through me...lets me know, whatever we had, we're never getting back.

It's been two days since I found out Sam was pregnant with my child, and possibly moving to another state. Christ, the moment I read that letter, it felt like my guts had been fillets with a dull butter knife. All the betrayal I'd ever felt came back and stole the air from my lungs, shattering the trust that had been growing between us.

I glance in my rearview mirror, and the sight of Daisy makes my heart pound harder. She's going to have a sibling. I'm still trying to wrap my brain around this insane turn of events. But isn't having a family with Sam something I had been thinking about? I hadn't been sure where she stood, and I had wanted to talk to her, to see if we could perhaps take our relationship to the next level.

But then I saw the letter. Talk about a kick to the teeth.

Then, if that wasn't enough, that positive pregnancy stick just about did me in. I may have wanted Sam in my life, wanted to make a family with her, but to think she went and got pregnant without even consulting me, well...that's some fucked-up shit.

She's not like that.

I suck in a sharp breath as that thought pings around inside my rattled brain, and while there is a part of me that believes she's kind, sweet and trustworthy, there's another part of me that's fucking scared.

"Daddy," Daisy says, and I catch her pout.

"Yeah, kiddo," I say in my happiest voice, despite the train wreck that I've become. Fuck man, I need to get my shit together. I have a child to think about.

"I miss Sam," she whines.

Me too.

The truth is, I miss her so fucking much, I can't even function. My mind goes back to all the time I spent with her. My heart beats faster, crashes against my chest. In the heat of the moment I reacted, said some pretty shitty things as my past came back to haunt me. I pinch my eyes shut as the vision of Sam fill's my mind's eye—her sweet smile, her generous nature. Why didn't she tell me she was leaving, and with my child?

Maybe she's not.

As that thought hits, I go over the events again. Truthfully, I'm not sure what is really going on anymore, but one thing I do know, is I need to talk to Sam, and this time I need to listen instead of jumping to all the worst conclusions, because that's exactly what I did.

We stop in front of the daycare, and I park. Daisy waves to Scotty, who's playing in the yard. Quinn, tanned from her long weekend in Mexico, glances up when she sees me, and her expression changes, the smile falling from her face.

I climb from the car, unbuckle Daisy, and guide her to the fenced-in yard, where kids are running around and playing on various pieces of equipment.

Quinn says something to one of her employees, gives Daisy a hug, and walks up to me.

"Let's go," she says.

"Go where?" I ask.

"Get in the car, Zander." The chill in her voice is enough to frost my windows.

I stare at her for a second, confused by the way she's acting. "Don't you have to be here with the kids?"

She jerks her thumb out. "My assistants are qualified to watch the kids in my absence. Now get in."

I climb into the driver's seat and she gets in beside me, slamming her door with much more force than necessary. "Where to?" I ask, having no idea what's going one or why she's acting like she's so pissed off at me.

Correction, she's not acting. She's completely and utterly pissed off at me. I never told her about Sam, so unless they had a conversation...

Ah, of course. That's it. The two had undoubtedly talked. They are, after all, friends. Such good friends, my sister tried to set her up with her bartender friend, Todd.

Anger boils in my blood at the image of Sam with another other man. I don't like it. I don't like it one fucking bit.

Jesus, I am so fucked up.

"There's a coffee shop, just around the corner."

"I know it," I say and pull into traffic. At the light, I take a left and drive a few more feet until the coffee shop is in view. I glance at Quinn, but she's staring straight ahead, her gaze trained on the road. I ease my car into a parking spot, and she jumps out and darts into the coffee shop ahead of me. I follow her in, and Jonah waves us both over.

What the fuck is going on? Am I walking in to some kind of intervention?

Oh, fuck...I think I am.

I stop dead in my tracks. "What's going on?" I ask.

"Sit," Jonah says, and gestures to the cup of coffee waiting for me.

I hesitantly lower myself, take a drink from the takeout cup, and wait to see what this is all about.

"Sam is pregnant," Quinn blurts out.

I take another sip and lower the cup. I fiddle with the plastic lid and meet my sister's gaze straight on. "She told you?"

"Yes, she told me. She's a wreck, Zander. And by the looks of things so are you." She shakes her head, her gaze slowly moving over me. "God, when was the last time you combed your hair or shaved your face?"

I run my hand over my chin, and the bristles rustle.

Quinn points a finger and waves it up and down the length of me. "Look at your clothes."

I glance down, and note the spaghetti stains on last night's T-shirt. "Yeah, okay. I could use a shower and change of clothes."

"If you love her, what's the problem here?" Quinn asks.

My head jerks up. "Who says I love her?"

"I do," Jonah pipes in, and folds his arms across his chest like he's daring me to challenge him.

"So do I," Quinn adds. "Look, I set her up with Todd on purpose. Todd is *gay*, Zander. He has a boyfriend."

"What the hell?"

"He was doing me a favor. I wanted to see your reaction, and dammit, you nearly went caveman on the guy! And don't think for a second that I don't know what went on in that bathroom. Everyone was talking about it after you left." She gives a low, slow whistle. "You've got it bad for her."

I sink back into my chair and run my hand through my hair. "Did she tell you she was leaving? That she's interviewing for a job in Texas?"

"Do you really believe that?" Quinn asks, and takes a pull from her cup, her eyes never leaving mine. "Did you stop for a second and listen to what she was trying to tell you?"

"No." For the millionth time, my mind goes back to the letter I found on Sam's kitchen table, to the horrible way I'd confronted her outside the bathroom. She'd started to say something but stopped when I noticed the stick. Was she trying to tell me she wasn't leaving and I was too stupid, too angry, to listen?

I briefly close my tired eyes. Fuck, I haven't slept properly in two days. "I don't know what to believe anymore." I only know Sam and I need to talk,

"Stop being such a chickenshit," Jonah says, and I glare at him, ready to punch him in the fucking mouth. Then again, I probably said the same thing to him, when he was fighting his own demons where my sister was concerned.

"I'm not a chickenshit," I say, and sit up a little straighter. I run my damp hands over my jeans and take deep breaths. Why does it feel like I'm suffocating in here?

Jonah scoffs, but then his eyes go serious. "No, what you are is a guy who cares so much about his daughter, he's shut everyone out. But it's not just your daughter you're protecting."

"You're protecting yourself too, Zander." Quinn reaches across the table, puts her hand over mine. "If anyone can understand what you're going through, how afraid you are of putting your heart out there, only to get it stomped on again, it's me."

I meet my sister's blue eyes, and a headache begins to brew at the base of my skull. I reach for my coffee with a shaky hand, but my throat is too tight to swallow. They're not wrong. The truth is, for many years now, I *have* been afraid. Too scared to trust, too afraid of getting hurt.

"Quinn..." I begin, and let my words fall off. I have no idea what to say, or where to go from here. All I know is I made a big mistake and somehow have to fix it.

"You love her, Zander," she says, a statement, not a question.

My heart squeezes, and I pinch the bridge of my nose as everything I feel for Sam wells up inside me, clogs my throat to the point of pain. "She's having my baby."

You were the one who first forgot the condom, dude.

"You're so afraid, you pushed her from your life before she could disappear from yours," Quinn says.

Jesus, when did my sister get so smart. I shake my head, so goddam proud of the woman she is today.

"It's time to stop pushing, Zander. Great things can happen when you do." She leans into Jonah, and he wraps his arms around her, the love they have for each other filling the space between us.

I swallow down the bile punching into my throat as I consider what she's saying to me. Had I sabotaged us on purpose? Had I left her before she could leave us?

"Do you honestly think Sam is the type of girl to trick you, use you to get a baby, and then disappear?" Quinn asks softly.

"No," I say with total confidence as I think about Sam, and the horrible things I said to her. Embarrassment, regret and shame fill me, and I don't try to tamp it down. I deserve to feel miserable. I lashed out from fear, and I fucking hate myself for it. She deserved better from me.

"Neither do I," Quinn says quietly.

"Fuck me," I say, and plant my elbows on the table. I press my palms into my eyes until I see stars. "What the fuck have I done?" My throat gurgles, and I take deep gulping breaths. When it comes right down to it, I'm no better than her other boyfriends, or her ex-fiancé. I blamed her for all of this, yet I was the one who forgot the condom that first time.

Sam is kind, compassionate...a woman who put her darkest secrets as well as her body into my hands. She is a woman to be trusted, one without a secret agenda. She opened herself up to Daisy and me, bringing us both into her childhood home, gifting us with family and friends and allowing us to be a part of something very special. Sam is a woman full of love and devotion, and Daisy and I, for a short time, were lucky enough to be a part of that.

What she *isn't* is a woman who ruins relationship.

No, the men in her life do that. They're responsible.

I'm responsible.

"I totally fucked up," I murmur around a tongue gone thick.

"Yeah, you did," Jonah says. "And now it's time to fix it."

"I'm sure she hates me. I was an asshole. Fuck, man, the things I said." I grip my coffee cup. "I even asked her if the baby was mine."

Jonah cringes, and whispers, "Jesus, that's bad."

"You need to talk to her," Quinn says. "Just like you, she's hurting, Zander."

"I never meant to hurt her. I...I love...love her," I say, tripping on my words as I allow my heart to fill with hope.

"I know."

"She's having my baby, Quinn," I say, as my pulse pounds hard against my throat.

She's having my baby.

"I love her," I say, allowing myself to get excited about the future. "I love her so fucking much."

Quinn grins at me and sits up a little straighter. "I don't think we're the ones you should be telling that to."

"She'd never...believe me. God, I was such a...a fucking prick." As I stumble over my words again, another thought hits—and I hate myself even more.

Christ, after I'd accused her of horrible things, she fought for her words...not because she was deceiving me or trying to come up with a lie, but because her stutter came back.

She wasn't hedging at all. I treated her like shit, and her voice faltered because her emotions got the better of her.

"If I were her, I'd never forgive me."

"You once told me you were a lover not a fighter, remember that?" Jonah asks.

"Yeah," I say. It was the day I'd told him to stop being an asshole and go fight for Quinn.

"It's time for you to be a fighter, Zander, and fight for what you want."

I take a deep breath and let it out slowly as an idea takes shape. "You're right." I'm not sure if what I'm about to do will work, but if I have to tie her to the bed and grovel until she accepts my apology and agrees to be mine, then so be it.

21

SAM

What the ever-loving fuck is going on?

I wake to bright sunshine streaming in though the crack in my curtain, but that's not what's giving me a pounding headache this early Saturday morning. No, it's the thunderous noise coming from outside.

Grumbling, because I'd wanted to sleep in after an emotional couple of days, I slide from my bed. My sheets, a tumbled mess from all my tossing and turnings, pool at the foot of my mattress.

Ever since my fight with Zander, I've not had a decent night's sleep. I put my hand on my stomach, and once again, tears well up inside me. I haven't even told my family about my pregnancy, and I'm not sure what the future holds for us, but I vow to my baby to be the best mother I can be.

Zander is an amazing father, and even though he doesn't want me, he said he'd fight for his rights. But he doesn't have to fight. I'm not about to keep his child away from him. I love him, and care for him, and no matter what he might have said to me, I would never strike back and use our child as a pawn.

Slowly, I make my way to the window and pull open the curtains.

I stand there, dumfounded, as huge tractors and other types of construction equipment fill my yard.

Another big bang hits the side of my house, and I nearly jump from my skin. That's when my sleep-deprived brain jolts awake, and understanding dawns.

There is a construction crew outside—and they're working on the wrong house!

Panicking, I tug on a pair of yoga pants, grab last night's T-shirt off the floor, and don't even bother combing my hair. I need to put a stop to this before they do any more damage and I'm responsible for repairs. Business might be picking up, but I have a long way to go before I can afford renovations to my home. I dress quickly, run to my front door, and swing it open.

"Hey," I yell, not to anyone in particular, but my voice is swallowed by the noisy equipment. I step outside and, bare-foot, I run around to the side of the house, where the most noise is coming from. Once there, I find a crew of men cutting into my exterior wall.

I gulp and wave my hands frantically. "Stop, please stop!"

"It's not safe for you to be out here, especially with no shoes on," a man says from behind.

My heart jumps into my throat at the sound of Zander's voice.

I spin around, and when I come face to face with him, my world goes a little fuzzy around the edges.

"What are you doing here?" I rush out. My God, it's the crack of dawn on a Saturday morning. Why would he be up and at my house so early?

Wait, has something happened?

"Where's Daisy?" I ask. "Is she okay?"

"Isn't that just like you." He waves his hand. "All this going on and your concerns are with Daisy." He takes a step toward me. "She's fine. She's with Quinn."

"Zander, what's going on? You need to help me stop these guys. They're tearing into the wrong house!"

"No, they're not," he says.

I shake my head, try to make sense of it all.

Zander puts his arm around my waist, and I let him lead me away. We step into the house, away from all the dangerous equipment and noise, and he closes the door behind us.

"What's going on?" I ask, planting my hands on my hips. "Why is there a construction crew tearing down my wall?"

"It's all part of our agreement, and I'm simply holding up my end of the deal."

"What deal?" I ask, unable to decipher his cryptic words this early in the morning.

"I told you, as long as we were together, I'd do repairs around your house. You wanted an exterior entrance to your office, and I hired the right people to do it. My skill set only goes so far," he says, his grin so adorable, it takes all my strength not to hurdle myself at him.

But then I remember where we stand.

My heart crashes a little harder in my chest as he hovers in my entranceway, his presence overwhelming me. "But we're not together," I remind him, and take a measured step back. Being close to him, feeling his heat, catching whiffs of his scent, it's all messing with my mind. "You accused me of some pretty horrible things, then walked out, remember?"

His nods, and his nostrils flare as he rakes a shaky hand through his mussed hair. Cripes, he looks like he hasn't slept in a week. At least he's in clean clothes, unlike me.

"Come with me," he says, and takes my hand. He leads me to the kitchen, and he reaches for two wine glasses. I blink, unable to figure out what's going on as he goes to my fridge and fills the crystal stemware with milk. "No alcohol. We have to think of the little one," he says as he fills the goblets.

I stand there staring at him, waiting for him to make the next move. He hands a glass to me and holds his up in a toast. Our eyes lock, hold, and I almost laugh—hysterically. I'm not worried about having bad sex for the next seven year, because I won't be having sex at all. How could I ever be with another man after him? He may have hurt me, but that doesn't mean I don't still love him.

"Never have I ever been such an asshole," he says.

I put my glass down, in no mood for games. "Zander—"

"Never have I ever made such a colossal mistake in my entire life," he continues.

His words pound against my ears, and I go still a moment, to mull over what he's saying to me. Silence takes up space between us as we stare at each other, and I finally break the quiet with, "I have to agree."

"Sam, this is all my fault," he says, his eyes so full of pain it softens something inside me. "I take full responsibility for everything. *Everything*—including the pregnancy."

"Pregnancy takes two people, Zander. You're not fully responsible."

He sets his glass down and takes my hands in his. "I ruined everything. Not you. I should have been better than the men you've had in your life. You deserve so much more from me." He glances at my belly. "So does our little one."

Oh my God, what is happening?

"The things I said to you...there was no excuse. You see, Sam, I wanted you in my life. I wanted for us to be together, and I wanted to have a family with you."

"Wanted?"

He cups my face, lightly brushes his thumb over my cheek as my pulse pounds against my ears. "I still want. I want all those things, with *you*."

"I...I want those things with you, too. I never...meant to get pregnant."

"I know that. I'm a dick for the things I said to you. I sabotaged us. Because I was scared. Because I—"

"I understand," I say, cutting him off as my heart swells, presses against my rib cage. "You had plenty of reasons to be afraid."

"But don't you see, I shouldn't have been afraid with you." He dips his head, his mouth close to mine. "Not with you, Sam. Never with you. You are the kindest, most honest woman I know. I swear to you, if you'll forgive me, I'll never be afraid again."

My pulse beats against my throat as my mind recalls all the cruel things he said, the things he accused me of. "You really hurt me."

"And I plan to spend the rest of my life making up for that. I want us to be together. I want this baby for us, for Daisy."

My gaze moves over his face, searches for signs of uncertainty. But I find none. "Are you really sure that's what you want? I don't want you to resent me down the road, or think I ever tried to trap you."

He picks up our glasses and hands one to me. "Never have I ever trusted anyone, or wanted to be with anyone, more than I want to be with you," he says. He holds his glass out and doesn't drink, because he's telling the truth.

I lift mine, bring it to my lips—and his mouth drops, deep worry taking up residency in his eyes. He knows if I drink, it means I've trusted someone more than I trust him. Wanted to be with someone more than I want to be with him.

I press the goblet to my lips, and his entire body tightens. He lids drop, and he clenches down on his back teeth with an audible click.

I let him suffer for a split second...then lower my glass.

His lids lift, his blue eyes full of hope and love as they move over my face. "Sam?"

"Never have I ever wanted to be with anyone more than I want to be with you." I say, and he lets loose a breath. "But I couldn't make it too easy on you, Zander. You did hurt me."

"Never make it easy on me, Sam." He exhales loudly once more, and holds his glass up again. "Never have I ever loved anyone the way I love you."

I don't take a drink, and he takes my glass from my shaky hand. He sets both goblets on the counter and pulls me in to his arms and kisses me deeply.

I hug him to me, absorb his warmth and comfort.

"I am so sorry, Sam. I want to take care of you, and love you the way you deserve to be loved. I want to help you around here, support you in your practice. I want you to move in with me, and if the commute becomes too much, we'll find you another location, or turn a part of my—or rather, our—place into a practice. Anything you want. But those are thoughts for another time. Right now, I'm asking for your forgiveness, even though I'm not sure I deserve it."

My heart soars as he lays his on the line. I can't stay mad at him. I love him with all my heart and then some. "I accept your apology."

"Hmmm," he says, his eyes narrowing like he's deep in thought.

"What?"

He cocks his head playfully. "I'm not sure how I feel about you accepting my apology so readily."

"Really?" I ask, confused, but I know he's up to something by the mischievous grin on his face.

"You see, I came here ready to tie you to the bed and grovel until you forgave me."

"Maybe there's still a part of me that's angry," I tease.

He scoops me up and carries me to my room. Once inside,

her sets me down and runs his knuckles over my cheek. "I love you, Sam."

"Never have I ever loved anyone the way I love you, Zander."

He presses his forehead to mine and blinks rapidly. His breath is coming a bit faster now. "Will you marry me, Sam? Will you be my wife, and Daisy's stepmother?"

"No," I say quickly.

His head jerks back, worry backlighting his gorgeous blue eyes. "No?"

"I don't want to be Daisy's stepmother."

"I...I'm sorry. Yeah, maybe that was pushing it. I guess, ah...you're not ready for that. You don't want a ready-made family. I think...I—"

"Zander," I say, and press my finger to his lips to quiet him. "I want to be your wife, and I want to be Daisy's *mother*, not her stepmother. I want us to be a real family. I want to legally adopt her."

He takes a shuttering breath, water pooling in his eyes. No longer able to hold back my own tears, I let them fall freely, and they slide down my cheeks and wet my T-shirt.

Zander sniffs and wipes at his face. "You're killing me here, Sam."

Laughing, I wrap my arms around him and kiss him deeply. "Now, what was this you were saying about tying me up?"

He picks me up, and I wrap my legs around him as he carries me to the bed. As he falls over me, kisses me with all the love and passion inside him—all the trust—it dawns on me that we didn't get what we once had back...but what we have here now is so much better.

AFTERWORD

Thank You!

Thank you so much for reading The Hard Hitter, book four in my Players on Ice series. I hope you enjoyed the story as much as I loved writing it. Please read on for an excerpt of His Obsession Next Door. Stay turned for more Players on Ice.

Interested in leaving a review? Please do! Reviews help readers connect with books that work for them. I appreciate all reviews, whether positive or negative.

Happy Reading,
Cathryn

HIS OBSESSION NEXT DOOR

"What's gotten into the puppies tonight?" Veterinarian Gemma Matthews asked her assistant as she finished securing the last howling pooch into its kennel.

Victoria gave a mock shiver and shot a nervous glance toward the shelter window. "It's the moon. It'll be full tomorrow night."

Despite the uneasy feeling mushrooming inside Gemma, she laughed at her assistant and followed the long column of silver moonlight illuminating a path along the cement floor. She reached the front lobby of her clinic, now eerily quiet after a demanding day of surgeries, and turned to Victoria. She gave a playful roll of her eyes, and said, "You've seen too many scary movies."

Victoria dabbed gloss to her lips, smacked them together and countered with, "Hey, it could happen."

Gemma arched a brow, humoring the young girl she'd hired straight out of veterinary college. "You think?"

"Sure." Victoria's long, blonde ponytail flicked over her shoulder as she gestured to the no-kill shelter attached to the clinic. "That's why the dogs are barking." Her green eyes widened and her voice sounded conspiratorial when she added, "They can sense the big, bad wolf out there, ready to shred a human's heart into a million tiny pieces."

"I hate to break it to you, Victoria," Gemma said, grinning at her assistant's antics, "but werewolves don't exist." Even though Gemma didn't believe in the supernatural, there was nothing she could do to ignore the jittery feeling that had been plaguing her all day. The truth was, the dogs weren't the only ones feeling antsy and out of sorts on this hot summer night.

Her assistant held her arms up and jangled the big, silver charm bracelets lining her wrists. "Well I'm not taking any chances, which is why I've armed myself with silver."

Before Gemma could respond, the office phone started ringing. As Victoria turned her attention to the caller, Gemma dimmed the lights and made her way to the front door to stare out into the ominous night. She stole a glance skyward and took in the mosaic of stars shimmering against the velvet backdrop. Even though the Austin night was calm, with not a cloud to be found in the charcoal sky, deep inside Gemma could sense a strange new ripple in the air. It left her feeling ill at ease. She placed a hand over her stomach, unable to shake the feeling that all was not right in her world.

Honestly, she had no reason to feel apprehensive or troubled, considering she finally had everything she ever wanted —her own clinic in the city, a no-kill shelter to help re-home animals, and an upcoming banquet that would hopefully raise enough funds to expand her animal sanctuary before she had to start turning pets away.

Swallowing down her edginess, Gemma set the deadbolt and was about to switch the sign from Open to Closed when a tall, dark figure stepped from the inky shadows. She sucked in a quick breath and felt a measure of panic as the very male, very *familiar* figure came into view.

Speaking of the big, bad wolf.

"Oh. My. God," she rushed out breathlessly.

"Is everything okay?" Victoria asked from behind the counter.

Instead of answering, Gemma's shaky hands went back to the deadbolt, certain she had to be hallucinating. The bell overhead jangled as she pulled the door open and the second she came face to face with the man from her past, the same man who'd rebuffed her seduction days after her seventeenth birthday, she feared nothing would ever be okay again.

Moving with the confidence of a man on a mission, he came closer, the long length of his powerful legs eating up the black sidewalk in record time. Even in the dark she'd recognized that hard body of his, developed from hardcore military training rather than endless hours in some sleek gym. Her gaze took in the leather motorcycle jacket stretched over broad shoulders before traveling back to his chiseled face. Dark, penetrating eyes—harder now from having seen too much carnage—locked on hers, and the raw strength of the impact hit like a physical blow.

He came barreling through her front door. "Gemma," he rushed out breathlessly. The urgency in his voice had the fine hairs on the back of her neck spiking with worry.

"Cole," she somehow managed to say around a tongue gone thick as she stumbled backward. "What...how...?" She choked on her words as she glanced past his shoulders to see where he'd come from. She'd been positive that after the funeral last year she'd never set eyes on this man again, and if she did, their chance meeting wouldn't go down like this.

Worried eyes full of dark concern cast downward. "Gemma...it's...it's Charlie...he's hurt..." Cole's fractured words fell off and that's when Gemma's gaze dropped.

Her heart leaped into her throat and she instantly snapped into professional mode when she caught the silhouette of the Labrador Retriever bundled in his arms. "Follow me." Jumping into action she turned and found Victoria rushing down the hall toward Exam Room 1, already a step ahead of them.

Gemma moved with haste and worked to quiet her racing heart. "Tell me exactly what happened." She kept her tone low and her voice controlled in an effort to calm Cole and minimize his anxiety.

Keeping pace, he followed close behind her, his feet tight on her heels. "We were out for a run in Sherwood Park," he began. "A squirrel sidetracked him, and he veered off the beaten path. He was jumping a log and didn't see the sharp branch sticking up."

She stole a quick glance over her shoulder and when dark, intense eyes focused on hers, her stomach clenched. "It's going to be okay, Cole. I promise." She drew a breath and gave a silent prayer that it was a promise she could keep. Gemma pushed through the swinging door and gestured with a quick nod toward the sterile examination table while she hurried to ready herself.

Understanding her silent command, Cole secured the whimpering dog onto the prep counter. Gemma's heart pinched when he placed a solid, comforting hand on the animal's head and spoke in soothing tones while Victoria went to work on preparing the pre-surgical sedative.

Gemma scrubbed in quickly and put on her surgery gear. She gave the dog a once-over before she dabbed at the blood to assess the depth of the wound. Angling her head, she cast Cole a quick glance. "Why don't you take a seat in the other room. This could take a while."

"I'm staying," Cole said firmly, their gazes colliding in that old familiar battle of wills.

Uncomfortable with the idea of him watching while she worked, and fully aware that he was a distraction she didn't need during surgery, she urged, "It could get messy."

"I've seen blood before, Gemma." With his feet rooted solidly, he folded his arms across his chest. "I'm not leaving him."

"Cole—"

"I'm fine."

Not wanting to waste time with a debate and knowing Cole was a bomb expert who'd seen his fair share of blood in the field, she gestured toward the chair in the corner. Once Cole stepped away, she cleansed the animal's wounds and continued her assessment.

She checked temperature, pulse and respiration before evaluating Charlie's gums. She shot Victoria a look as her assistant secured the blood pressure cuff and waited for the go ahead on the pre-surgical sedative.

"He's already trying to crash," Gemma said. "We have to go straight to surgery."

Working quickly, Gemma hooked the dog to an I.V. catheter and induced anesthesia while Victoria began the three-scrub process to shave and sterilize Charlie's skin.

Once the dog was clipped and scrubbed, Gemma reassessed. "He's lost a lot of blood, but I'm not seeing any visible organ damage. We'll have to flush the cavity to clean out the debris before we stitch."

As Gemma sprayed the area with warm saline, Victoria called out, "Pulse ox dropping, heart rate down to forty-five."

Damn, this was not good. Fearing she was missing something, she sprayed the area again and gave the cavity another assessment. That's when she noticed the tree had nicked a vessel on the liver. Gemma's heart leaped and worry moved through her as she exchanged a look with Victoria. Keeping her fingers steady and her face expressionless for Cole's sake, she worked quickly to tie the vessel off before it was too late. Once complete, she rinsed the area, and when the bleeding came to a halt, she exhaled a relieved breath.

She turned her attention to her suture. A long while later she glanced at the clock, noting that more than an hour had passed since Cole had first stepped foot in her door. Gemma secured the last stitch, wiped her brow and stood back to examine the dog.

"Vitals are good," Victoria informed her. Gemma gave a nod and took off her surgery garb. She quickly washed up and let loose a slow breath, confident that the dog would recover.

"Will he be okay?" Cole whispered.

Gemma's skin came alive, Cole's soft, familiar voice sending an unexpected curl of heat through her tired body. She turned to him and he stepped closer, the warmth of his body reaching out to her and overwhelming all her senses. As he looked at her with dark, perceptive eyes that knew far too many of her childhood secrets, she jerked her head to the right. "Let's go into the other room."

She pushed through the surgery doors and Cole followed her into the lobby where she could put a measure of distance between them.

"Is Charlie going to be okay?" Cole asked again, raking his hands through short, dark hair that had been cut to military standards.

Gemma rubbed her temples and leaned against the receptionist's counter. "He's lucky you got him to me when you did."

For the first time since stepping into her clinic, his shoulders relaxed slightly. "He's going to be okay?"

"Yes. He's going to be fine." She drew a breath and stared at the man before her, hardly able to believe that he was here in her clinic. Shortly after her botched seduction some ten years ago he'd enlisted in the army and had gone out of his way to avoid her.

As she considered that further, she decided to brave the question that had been plaguing her since he'd darkened her doorway. She waved her hand around the front lobby. "Why did you bring him here? There are other clinics closer to Sherwood Park."

Silence lingered for a minute, then in a voice that was too quiet, too careful, he said, "Because you were here, Gems, and I wouldn't trust Charlie's care in anyone else's hands but yours."

Her throat tightened at the use of his nickname for her, and while her heart clenched, touched at the level of trust he had in her, her brain cells made the next logical leap. "You've been back for a while, then," she stated in whispered words.

An expression she couldn't quite identify flitted across his face as he said, "A week now."

"Oh." Gemma shifted slightly, trying not to feel wounded that he'd been home for seven long days and hadn't even bothered to say hello.

She averted her gaze to shield the hurt but when he added, "I wanted to come sooner," she knew she could never hide anything from him.

She held her hand up to cut him off. "I understand how difficult this must be for you," she assured him, her mind going back to the last time they'd seen each other. Even though he'd been in a tremendous amount of pain at Brandon's memorial service, suffering as he said good-bye to his lifelong friend and fellow soldier, Cole had tried to console her, watching over her and taking care of her the same way he used to when they were kids.

It warmed her heart to know her brother hadn't died alone in the line of duty and that Cole had been there to care for him until the end. Her gaze panned his face. She took in the dark smudges beneath even darker eyes and couldn't help but wonder, who was taking care of him?

His eyes clouded as they stared blankly at some distant spot behind her shoulder. Hating the unmasked hurt on his face, as well as the awkwardness between them, she touched his arm. The air around them instantly changed. Cole flinched, his entire body tightening as if under assault. Gemma snatched her hand back, his rejection all too familiar. Even though she was all grown up now, a woman who wanted him as much today as she did all those years ago, he'd never see her as anything more than his friend's kid sister.

Just then the puppies broke out into a chorus of howls and Gemma couldn't help but wonder if they were on to something. Maybe the big, bad wolf did exist, and maybe she was staring at him. Perhaps she should heed Victoria's warning and arm herself with silver. There was no doubt that if she wasn't careful the man looming close could shred her heart into a million tiny pieces.

———

The second Gemma had touched his arm she lit a dangerous fuse inside him. Cole had immediately disengaged, knowing it could only end up backfiring and blowing up in his face. He hated the familiar hurt in her eyes when he recoiled, hated that he'd put it there—again—but he knew nothing good could come from the firestorm inside him, one that had been brewing since their youth. Gemma had tried to hide the pain, the hurt on her face, and she might have succeeded with someone who didn't know her the way he did.

"Gems," he whispered. He clenched his fingers and fought the natural inclination to pull her to him and comfort her like he did when they were younger. But if her body collided with

his—one part in particular—she'd know how she affected
him. And he couldn't let that happen. He had to stay strong.

Instead of acting on his needs, he took that moment to
pan her pretty features, noting the way she'd tied her long,
chestnut hair back into a ponytail. His gaze left her face to
trail over the supple swell of her breasts as they pressed
against her V-neck top. He shifted, uncomfortable as he
perused her slim waist and the way her sensuous curves
turned a pair of green surgery scrubs into a Victoria's Secret
spread. Christ, she was even more beautiful now than she was
when they were kids. But no matter what, and no matter how
he felt about her, when it came to Gemma, there was a line
he wasn't going to cross.

Her assistant came out from the back room. "He's stable
and ready to go to ICU." When her words met with silence,
her gaze tennis balled between the two, a sure sign that she
felt the tension in the room every bit as much as Cole did.
"Ah...Danielle will be here shortly. If you guys want to go, we
can finish up."

Gemma exhaled slowly and pushed off the counter.
"Thanks, Victoria. I'll come in early to check on him."

Cole stiffened. "He has to stay the night?"

"He   needs   to   be   monitored   for   at   least
twenty-four hours."

"Then I'm staying."

"It's not necessary. My night assistant will be here shortly,
and I'm on call twenty-four seven. He's resting soundly and
by the looks of you, you should be doing the same."

After a long moment, he gave a nod of agreement and
Victoria slipped into the back, leaving them alone once again.
Cole turned his full attention to Gemma and stretched his
neck, working the night's tension from his shoulders.

Moving with an innocent sensuality, she walked around
the counter to grab her purse from the drawer. Cole became

fully aware of the woman standing before him and exactly what she meant to him. He shifted on his feet and tore his gaze away, looking for a distraction before his mind took him back to that hot summer night when she'd lured him into the barn nestled at the back of her old homestead. Christ, it had taken all his effort not to lay her onto the soft bed of hay and take what he wanted.

But at seventeen she was a kid, as well as the younger sister of his closest friend. Of course, those weren't the only things stopping him from acting on his urges. No, when his own parents had been emotionally absent—too busy looking for happiness in the bottom of a bottle—her folks had practically taken him in. Cole would never be disloyal to the family who'd treated him like a son by sleeping with their only daughter.

"It's late and it's dark. Why don't you let me walk you home," Cole said, breaking the uncomfortable silence hovering like the sharp blade of a guillotine.

In typical Gemma fashion, she straightened her shoulders in that old, familiar way that let him know he'd hit a soft spot. "I'm capable of walking home by myself." She lifted her head a little higher. "In case you haven't noticed, I'm all grown up."

Oh, he'd noticed all right.

She opened her mouth to say something else, but he countered with, "It's on my way, Gems."

That gave her pause. Her head jerked back with a start and he didn't miss the accusation in her tone when she said, "Let me get this straight, you know where I work *and* where I live?"

"Yeah," he said, for lack of anything else.

Her big blue eyes narrowed. "Why is it you know so much about me yet I know nothing about you?"

"What do you want to know?"

Without hesitating she asked, "If walking me home is on your way, where do you live?"

He gestured to the motorcycle parked at the curb outside. "For now I've got a cot in the back of Freedom Cycle."

Perfectly manicured brows knit together as she angled her head curiously. "You're staying with Jack?"

"You remember Jack?"

She nodded. "Ex-sniper. Brandon always liked him." At the mention of her brother she rubbed the back of her neck and a contemplative look came over her face before she began again. "When I moved into one of my parents' downtown apartments during college Brandon told me—" she paused to do air quotes before saying, "—*Jack of all trades* was my go-to guy if I ever needed anything. I've run into him a couple of times since the funeral."

Cole paused for a moment before saying, "He takes in ex-soldiers and gives them work until they get back on their feet again."

"What I heard..." Her voice fell off and her eyes widened. "Wait... Are you saying...?"

"Yeah. I'm getting out, Gems. My days serving overseas will soon be behind me."

"Oh," she said, a mixture of surprise and relief swimming in her big blue eyes. Then she frowned. "So you're sleeping in the back of his shop?"

"Just until my new place is ready."

"And when will that be?"

"Tomorrow."

"Where will you be moving?"

Gemma stifled a yawn, and Cole could see exhaustion pulling at her. Instead of answering, he said, "Come on, I'm taking you home." He tossed her a lopsided grin, one that always pulled a smile from her when they were younger. "You know, for old time's sake."

Their eyes met and everything in his gut told him her thoughts were traveling down the same path as his. She too was remembering her youth and all the times he'd taken her home and snuck her to her room so she wouldn't get busted by her older brother or her folks. Sure, he'd lectured her on the dangers of her rebellious nature, but he'd always had an inherent need to protect her, from everyone and everything. He couldn't bring himself to let her get caught, even though it might have been for her own good. Then again, as long as he was around and watching over her, no harm would ever come to her.

"Cole—" she began, but he cut her off.

"I know, I know. You're quite capable of taking care of yourself," he said to appease her protest. He still wasn't taking a chance with her safety now that she was living on her own in the downtown core and he was back from overseas. Besides, when Brandon was dying in his arms and there wasn't a thing Cole could do to save him, he'd asked only one thing of Cole. And no matter what, Cole planned to follow through with the vow he'd made to Gemma's brother on that dark night, because he never, ever wanted to fail Brandon again.

ABOUT CATHRYN

New York Times and *USA today* Bestselling author, Cathryn is a wife, mom, sister, daughter, and friend. She loves dogs, sunny weather, anything chocolate (she never says no to a brownie) pizza and red wine. She has two teenagers who keep her busy with their never ending activities, and a husband who is convinced he can turn her into a mixed martial arts fan. Cathryn can never find balance in her life, is always trying to find time to go to the gym, can never keep up with emails, Facebook or Twitter and tries to write page-turning books that her readers will love.

Connect with Cathryn:
Newsletter
https://app.mailerlite.com/webforms/landing/c1f8n1
Twitter: https://twitter.com/writercatfox
Facebook:
https://www.facebook.com/AuthorCathrynFox?ref=hl
Blog: http://cathrynfox.com/blog/
Goodreads:
https://www.goodreads.com/author/show/91799.Cathryn_Fox

Pinterest http://www.pinterest.com/catkalen/

Hands On

Body Contact

Full Exposure

Dossier

Private Reserve

House Rules

Under Pressure

Big Catch

Brazilian Fantasy

Improper Proposal

Boys of Beachville

Good at Being Bad

Igniting the Bad Boy

Bad Girl Therapy

Stone Cliff Series:

Crashing Down

Wasted Summer

Love Lessons

Wrapped Up

Eternal Pleasure Series

Instinctive

Impulsive

Indulgent

Sun Stroked Series

Seaside Seduction

Deep Desire

Private Pleasure

Captured and Claimed Series:

Yours to Take

Yours to Teach

Yours to Keep

Firefighter Heat Series

Fever

Siren

Flash Fire

Playing For Keeps Series

Slow Ride

Wild Ride

Sweet Ride

Breaking the Rules:

Hold Me Down Hard

Pin Me Up Proper

Tie Me Down Tight

Stand Alone Title:

Hands on with the CEO

Torn Between Two Brothers

Holiday Spirit

Unleashed

Knocking on Demon's Door

Web of Desire